JOURNEY
of
DREAMS

For Tomasa. Thank you for whispering
your story in my ear and speaking to my heart.

Journey of Dreams copyright © Frances Lincoln Limited 2009
Text copyright © Marge Pellegrino 2009

First published in Great Britain and the USA in 2009 by
Frances Lincoln Children's Books, 4 Torriano Mews,
Torriano Avenue, London NW5 2RZ.
www.franceslincoln.com

The author wishes to thank the following for their help with this book: Marianna;
Amy; Vicky, Juana, Herminia, Catalina and Roberto, Laurie, Sebastian, Flor,
Patty and Wendy; all those who took part in the Sanctuary Movement;
Steve, Evan and Kathy; the Hopi Foundation, CPRV and Owl and Panther communities;
GUAMAP and St. Michael's Guatemalan Project; Kay, Fran, Gerry, Lynne, Juanita,
Judy, Carol, Charlene, Cornelia, Meg and Mel; Kendra; and Yvonne.

Cover illustration by David Dean

British Library Cataloguing in Publication Data available on request

ISBN 978-1-84780-061-9

Set in Aldus LT

Printed in Singapore

3 5 7 9 8 6 4 2

JOURNEY of DREAMS

MARGE PELLEGRINO

F

FRANCES LINCOLN
CHILDREN'S BOOKS

INTRODUCTION

"You can't know how we feel," Herminia, a refugee friend said, the night I went to her family's home to check some facts.

I agreed. There are many reasons why I can never know how Tomasa, my character, and this flesh-and-blood Herminia before me would feel. When I moved from Tuckahoe, New York to Tucson, Arizona it was my own choice. Refugees don't have that choice. They have to move to stay alive. I am not indigenous. I am not Guatemalan. I have not travelled the road Tomasa and her family walked.

But I have worked, laughed and cried with people who travelled a similar path. I read the case of a young Central American girl who was wounded and hid in a field all night. I saw the drawings she used to describe her experience. Later she came to Tucson for reconstructive surgery and stayed with my friends who talked to me about her story.

I know some of the brave people who worked in the Sanctuary Movement, who put their freedom on the line to save a stranger.

When Tomasa began whispering her story in my ear, I felt compelled to record her words.

In the highlands of Guatemala, each village was different. Every person who lived at that time had their own experience. But the truth lies in the places where these stories overlapped. It was from that rich soil that Tomasa's story grew.

I wrote this book in the hope of bringing a better understanding of unfamiliar people and situations. And I hope that readers will recognise Tomasa's braveness, and maybe even be inspired by her story to walk a little more bravely on their own journeys.

Marge Pellegrino

The family in this story lives in the Guatemalan highlands where they speak their native language K'iche' (Quiché) and some Spanish.

The Highlands of Guatemala, Central America, 1984

CHAPTER 1

Thwap, thwap, thwap. The high green branches of the pine trees shiver in the wind from the dark green machine whirring above us. My brother Carlos scoops up Manuelito and runs towards me. With his arm around my shoulder, we flee from the dark shadow, which moves swiftly along the ground. As we approach, Mama sees us and pulls back into our *ni'tzja*. We follow her inside our home. Together we sit on the floor, surrounded by the rest of our family. We sit without speaking, until the sound fades and the sun leaves us.

Our family does not talk about the helicopter that slashes the air like a machete. Instead, Papa strikes a match and lights the lamp. He takes on the voice of a storyteller and makes our fear vanish.

"Just before our first child was born, the mice paced back and forth on the roof of our *ni'tzja*, waiting for word of the birth. This house had male person" –

Papa points to himself – "and two females." He nods towards Mama and her mother, our grandmother, Abuela.

"It was not a friendly house for mice, because the women chased them and hid the food from them. The mice were so undernourished, they were easily caught and thrown out."

Abuela claps, as though she were catching a mouse in mid-air. "Those mice were not captured because they were starving and too slow," she boasts, "The women of this house were too fast for them!"

I laugh at Abuela, whose swollen legs keep her sitting down most of the time. Mama and I clap and catch an imaginary mouse too.

Papa smiles and then continues. "The mice who dared live in this *ni'tzja* were skinny mice. Our watchful women kept them on the run. Only one man was careless and dropped seeds for them to snatch. They could only hope that another male would be born to this house, to improve their chances of a better life.

"And so, on the night our first child was born, the lookout mouse climbed on to the roof and parted the thatch and looked down. He squeaked out the good news. The mice celebrated. Our Carlos had been born."

I look at Carlos, sitting on his mat. Carlos looks so much like Papa, with a strong nose and eyes as black as a cave. Their faces are both angular and pointed like the tips of stars.

"The mice danced all night to celebrate their good fortune. The house was now even – two males and two females."

Carlos smiles at our younger brother, Manuelito, who rests his head on Carlos' knee.

Manuelito hardly blinks. He walked far today, gathering flowers and roots for Abuela. Sleep is near, but I can see that he fights to stay awake. Soon he will become part of the story.

Papa turns towards me. "Tomasa, when the lookout mouse saw that another female had been born, he was greatly disappointed. That night there was no dancing for the mice. They went to bed early and cried."

I slap my hands, as if catching another mouse, as I always do at this part of the story. The sound of it helps Manuelito to stay awake. He knows he is next in the story, and sits up.

"Ah, but then our baby Maria arrived," Papa begins. He always teases Manuelito like this.

"Papa, what about me?" Manuelito complains.

Papa scratches his head. "Carlos," he says as he puts out one finger. Then, "Tomasa." And he puts out another. He looks up as if he has just discovered his blunder. "Oh, thank you for noticing my mistake," he says.

Now it is Mama who smiles, as Papa resumes the story.

"After Tomasa was born, several of the mice's ribs began to show. They were so scrawny. They could only light their tiny candles and pray that the odds would be better for them the next time.

"And soon Mama gave them hope again. Her stomach began to swell like the fruit on the trees. She gave birth to Manuelito – a boy. The mice could see from his strong arms and legs that he would work hard in the fields with his papa and brother Carlos. They knew more corn would grow in the field of this family now that Manuelito had arrived. And corn was their favourite food, just as it is the favourite food of the Mayan. Once again, there was an equal number of males and females, and the mice were satisfied."

Content, Manuelito settles down on to his mat. Before Papa gets to the mice's disappointment at Maria's birth, Manuelito is asleep.

"And the mice have decided to move on now that Maria has arrived."

Abuela reaches out and smoothes Maria's soft tufts of black hair.

I lie down as Papa finishes his story. I listen to the others breathe as I slide closer to sleep.

In my dream, mice scramble to hide from an owl, which hoots nearby.

I wake as Papa rises from his mat and slips outside in to the night. The owl is not a dream. I hear it again, and get up to follow Papa. He looks towards the village. I scan the dark shadows in the other direction.

Hooo. Hooo, hoo. Hooo. Papa and I both turn to the sound. I see the silhouette of the largest of the owls that live in our mountains perched on the top of a pine tree. Papa picks up a rock.

Hooo. Hooo, hoo. Hooo comes from a tree behind us. We turn round.

Carlos joins us in the dark as we stand between the owls. The flesh on my arms rises up like hundreds of tiny anthills. I shudder. Owls kill rats that destroy our crops, but we know that when the owl comes, death and sadness follow.

Papa throws a rock at the centre of the tree where the first owl sits. I hear the rustling of a branch and the thud of the rock hitting the trunk, followed quickly by a smaller thud when the rock hits the earth. I hear the whish of wing against air as the owl swoops down and floats just hands above our heads. He slices the air like a helicopter, climbs again to the top of the tree and lands next to the other owl.

Hooo. Hooo, hoo. Hooo, they tell each other.

Papa throws another rock.

Together the owls fly out of sight. I pray that they take their trouble with them.

✿ ✿ ✿

Back inside, on my mat, I wait for sleep to find me
again.

In my dream, my friend Catarina shouts. "Alto!"

I stop short.

We play statues, freezing at each cry of "alto".

*But in my dream my statue arms do not freeze.
They sprout deep green feathers like the quetzal's
wings. The red feathers of my bird-breast flash. I fly.
Together Catarina and I soar over wooden thatched
houses. Under our wings, we see paths paint the earth
brown, connecting each of the thirty-seven houses to
the village plaza, where the church sits.*

*We land in front of my family's ni'tzja. I see Mama
inside. In slow motion, she sprinkles the dirt floor with
water to keep the dust down. The drops scatter on their
way from her fingertips to the floor, reflecting the sun
in mid-air, shining like tiny rainbows. Mama turns
and smiles when she sees me.*

*And in an instant I am in her arms. She hugs me
close. I feel the gentle weave of her shawl against my
cheek. I smell sweet yellow flowers from the jungle
and smoke from fire of the comal. She whispers my
name, "Tomasa," and my heart fills.*

*And then a shadow swoops down and I dive out
of Mama's arms to hide from the owl's outstretched*

talons. *The thwap, thwap, thwap gets louder and louder. The owl has become the helicopter.* "Mama!" *I shout in my dream, as I see the dark green machine's side open. I pull Mama down with me to avoid the gun pointing at us from the sky.*

✿ ✿ ✿

I wake with a pounding heart. *Que'cj a'k* crows his rooster's morning song. I hear Mama get up, watch her part her waist-long black hair. She braids each side with the strip of red cloth I wove for her on my loom.

Maria stretches herself awake. I take her to Abuela, who makes Maria laugh while I help Mama warm the small *tamales* we made yesterday.

After breakfast, Papa and Carlos cross the road and go into the field. Moon-faced Manuelito searches the land behind our *ni'tzja* to find the flowers and roots Abuela needs. Mama sprinkles the floor to keep down the dust, just as I dreamed.

I help tie up the bundles with our herbs and the cloth we have woven for market. I grab my shawl and wrap it around my shoulders.

The early morning mist is already rising as I rush outside to meet the truck rattling towards our house. Even before the brakes squeal the wheels to a stop, I am standing by the road. Before the horn beeps and the engine coughs and goes silent, I am ready to ride with my friend into town to market.

I look down at my toes in the dirt. They peep out from under my skirt, the first I ever wove for myself. I wiggle my toes as Catarina's brother Hector jumps out from the bed of the truck. He races to meet Carlos, who has just emerged from the green of our field.

In the back of the truck, Catarina smiles wide and reaches over the back rail to take my bundle. I notice how her blouse has grown tight against her chest. Only three years separate us, yet at sixteen she looks like a woman, while I still look like a child at thirteen.

"Manuelito!" Mama calls. My younger brother appears from behind the house with yellow flowers in his hands. He runs inside to deliver them to Abuela, who will use them to make a light brown tea for the swelling in her legs. Manuelito charges back outside as I step up on to the chinkered chrome bumper of the faded black truck. I settle in the back next to Catarina.

Manuelito squirms as Carlos lifts him up.

"I can climb in by myself."

"Of course you can, Monkey," Carlos says, and puts him back down on the road.

"Can I walk with you?" Manuelito asks.

"Oh, but then you would be too tired to play your best when you get to town," Carlos says, turning to leave. "See you later!" Carlos calls to us, as he and Hector walk down the road.

When it's clear Carlos won't change his mind, Manuelito climbs into the truck.

Mama joins us from the house. Our little Maria's head pokes over Mama's shoulder from where she is secured in Mama's shawl. Mama calls after Carlos, "Take care son," – *K'awilawib* – something she now says to us whenever we leave her. She puts her bundle in the back.

Mama frees Maria from her shawl and kisses her before she hands her over to me.

Maria reaches out to Mama. She still wants Mama to hold her, even though she is a year old.

"Sit with me," I tell my sister.

Catarina shakes Maria's small hand, "Nice to see you, Hummingbird."

Maria relaxes as I lightly stroke the back of her head.

Mama smiles. Once she sees that Maria will stay with us, she climbs up into the cab and sits beside Catarina's mother, who starts up the engine. We wave to Abuela, who waves back from the doorway with the yellow flowers in her hand. She has folded a red and blue *tzut* and fastened it on to her head as though she, too, were going to market.

The truck bounces and rocks down the road through our family's field. We wave to Abuela until she disappears behind the corn that now stands taller than the top of the truck. I notice around the feet of the corn that the squash's buds have grown fat. My mouth waters at the thought of eating those pale orange flowers. We will pick them in the next few days. Before we do, I will weave their design with the threads of my backstrap loom.

We slow down as we pass Carlos and Hector running past the last houses in our village. Four older boys have joined their race.

"*K'awilawib*," Mama calls out the window. 'Take care' has taken on a new meaning since the soldiers came.

"See you later, snails," Catarina calls.

The boys stop. As soon as I see Hector flick a match to wake the flame, I know what he is about to do. I cover Maria's ears.

He throws fireworks through the dust that swirls behind us on the road. The burst of pops rips the air and erupts behind the truck.

Maria jumps in my lap and squeezes my arms. Manuelito smiles and claps his hands.

"Mama bought those firecrackers for the *fiesta*," Catarina shouts at her brother. The boys laugh as the distance between us grows. "No more fireworks!" she shouts.

Hector lights one more and throws it towards us.

"Stop wasting the matches!" Catarina yells.

Even Maria laughs with us at the final pop.

As we turn on to the main road, we lose sight of our brothers. They will cut through the fields and get there in half the time.

We stop to pick up a family from our village. We are wedged so tightly in the back of the truck that I feel like fruit in a basket. The main road has almost as many ruts as the village road. Maria's head wobbles with the rhythm of the truck.

Before we have gone far, an army truck roars up behind us. Everyone in our truck looks down. Catarina and I cover most of our faces with our shawls.

The army truck pulls up next to us and we ride in the cold of its shadow.

My heart races. I turn my head in the other direction and hold Maria close, wishing I could be invisible to the eyes peering at us. "Monkey," I say to Manuelito, to remind him not to stare. He does not want to turn into one of the monkeys who shrieks from the tree-tops like the disobedient children in a story Papa tells us. Manuelito looks down at his knees bent up against his chest.

A horn blares. I look up. Through the windshield I see another truck coming towards the army truck. Instead of pulling in behind us, the truck continues along beside us – straight towards the other truck.

I tighten my grip on Maria with one hand and hold on to the side of the truck with the other. A second before the trucks crash, the other truck swerves off the road.

As we pass, I see that the swerving truck has lost part of its load. The driver gets out to retrieve what has fallen.

Surely the soldiers will see that we are not the guerrillas, the *g'oy* who, they say, cause trouble! They must understand we are just *ajchaquib'*, people from the village who are on our way to the market to sell what we grow and weave, what we gather and cook and build.

They must have realised this, because finally the army truck drives off.

✿ ✿ ✿

When we reach the market, I help Mama spread her blanket. While she hugs Manuelito and releases him to go off to play with his friends, I arrange the red, white and yellow belts Mama has woven. She is known for her elaborate coloured patterns which have a life of their own and do not always conform to the traditional patterns of our village. I set out the belts I have made in a separate line. Although the difference in our work is clear to anyone walking by, mine now look good enough to bring in money. Last month, two of mine sold. I am glad to be able to help pay our school fees. Not every child in the village has our good luck and can go to school.

"What a beautiful *huipil*," the cheese-seller says as I lay out Mama's colourful blouses. Each time we come to market, this woman stops to admire Mama's work. "One day," she says, "when the design is just how I imagined it, I will buy one."

"What do you imagine?" Mama asks, as she does each time they talk. Every time, the woman describes something different. Each month Mama weaves a *huipil* with a design the woman has described the time before – hummingbirds drinking from blossoms, or *quetzals* seen sideways with their long tail feathers curling, or a braid of flowers that heal, looking as fresh as they are the moment when Manuelito discovers them in the forest.

"The gold stripes sing against the blue," the woman says, "but this is not quite what I had in mind." And she never buys a *huipil* from Mama, but someone else always buys the one the woman has described.

Before Mama finds out which design the woman would like next time, I excuse myself. I take the bundle of herbs and dried flowers Abuela has prepared to trade for soap.

I do not stay long at the stalls as I sometimes do,

looking at everything for sale. Instead, I hurry around the square, past the shoes, hats and baskets. I linger a moment at the bright fists of yarn piled up in all the colours of the rainbow. I stop to check the price of fireworks for the fiesta, in case Mama sells enough for us to buy some.

And then I find the soap woman. I pick up a bar and inhale the smell of pine from the green soaps with flecks of red from the flowers Abuela sent last time. I hand the woman the flowers after she has wrapped two bars of black soap. It is made with ash and pig fat. We have not had a pig to cook and eat since before Maria was born.

By the time I get back, the boys have arrived. Carlos is leading a cow off the pasture they use for playing football. Hector follows, swatting the top of the cow's back leg with his flat hand. The other boys shout and clap their hands at the sheep to shoo them away.

"*Gracias*, Tomasa," Mama says, taking the soap. "Thank you. Now go and have fun." I wave goodbye to Maria, who chews on one of my belts as she sits on the blanket next to Mama.

✧ ✧ ✧

Catarina and I stand watching the football with other girls and young boys from the surrounding villages. Several children play jacks with stones they have picked up and a small white ball from the market. I watch the smile on Catarina's face. Her eyes follow the boy who will soon be her husband, as he runs down the field.

"Bravo!" Catarina and I call out. We laugh and clap when he jumps over a sheep and scores a goal, in spite of the woolly intruder who has wandered back on to the football field. As the players chase it away, Hector's eyes seek me out.

I blush. I should have looked down sooner. I have never been so bold before.

While the older boys play, Manuelito and his young friends imitate them on the sidelines. They kick the ball to each other, clumsily weave and pass as they drive the ball towards a goal made from a discarded box.

When the older boys' game is over, Hector and Carlos play with the young boys. My family starts to gather in the market square where Mama sits. She hands us each a few of the small *tamales*, and we listen to the boys telling about their games as customers walk by.

"Are you too tired to go with us, Manuelito?" Carlos asks. My younger brother's eyebrows shoot up and his black eyes grow bigger. He looks as though he cannot believe the good news he hears. Mama smiles and nods her approval to Carlos. Her eyes make a silent plea for them to take care.

"How much for the *huipil* with the blue and gold stripes?" a man asks, as we start packing up our things.

Mama talks to him while I watch Hector, Manuelito and Carlos growing smaller and smaller in the distance.

✿ ✿ ✿

When we get home and out of the truck, Catarina says, "Watch out. The boys might be hiding in the corn."

I feel a bit disappointed that they don't jump out to scare us.

"Hector!" Catarina calls towards the field. She wants to start work on her loom. She sold two of her woven shawls today and hopes to sell twice as many before the *fiesta*.

Her mother sounds two short bursts on the truck's horn. When the boys still don't appear, Catarina gets into the cab with her mama.

"*Adios*, Tomasa," she says, as they drive off.

We put what we did not sell in the corner by my sleeping mat. Mama starts the fire for the evening meal while I pick up some thread and start on my weaving. Maria sits next to Abuela, chewing on her doll's foot. I hear a loud scratching in the thatch above me – a squirrel, maybe.

Through the open door, the late afternoon sun deepens the blue of the sky. At this moment of the day, the green of the field and pine trees beyond glow. The blue and the green next to each other look magical. The green crops grow from the gifts of the sky and earth. And we, the people of the corn, grew from those crops. Maybe that is why I often weave blue and green next to each other.

Over the rustle of the corn in the breeze, I hear running. The short quick stride says it must be Manuelito. He runs fast. He must be racing with Carlos, whom I do not hear. I smile at Carlos and Hector, who must be letting him win.

Manuelito bursts in. His red, tear-streaked face speaks fear. He runs to Mama; he holds her.

"What, son? What?" Mama asks. I peep out of the door. The road is empty.

Manuelito answers, but I cannot understand his words muffled in her waist. Mama pulls him back from her and looks at his face.

"Tell me again, son."

And when he repeats the words, my heart pounds.

"Soldiers," he sobs. "Soldiers took Carlos and Hector."

I run through green rows of corn until my lungs scream for me to slow down.

"Papa!" I shout. No answer. I run again. I call for him a second and third time. Finally he calls back and when we reach each other, I tell him what has happened. He drops his hoe with a thud on to the ground.

"Tell me again," Papa says. When I finish, he pushes his straw hat up on his forehead. He touches the thin moustache above his lip.

"Where did they go?"

"Manuelito said back towards the market."

Papa turns and runs. I follow. He slows down, and calls over his shoulder, "Go home, Tomasa."

I stand motionless surrounded by growing things. I wait for them to whisper that it is all a mistake, but I hear only leaves touching leaves. I pick up the hoe and turn to walk home.

CHAPTER 2

Outside our *ni'tzja*, I lean the hoe against the wall.

Inside, Mama moves her hands as though grinding corn is the one thing that keeps her heart inside her chest. She bore other children between me and Manuelito, but I do not remember them. Another one came between Manuelito and Maria. When we put the baby in the earth with the others, Mama's face looked as it does now.

Abuela has taught me to calm myself with my breathing. I fill myself quietly with air and release it slowly. When I was young, this breathing was just a game. But now I see that my outward calmness is a help to Mama.

She puts us to work. She sends Manuelito to cut up firewood and feed the goat and chickens. I separate the dried corn from the cobs.

I tell my fear over and over: *be still*, until I am quiet enough to pray, as I know Abuela and Mama are praying. We may not be using the same words, but we all yearn for the same thing. As the kernels fall into the basket, I pray to Our Lady of Guadalupe: *Please bring them back. Bring them home.* Maria reaches for any stray kernels that bounce on the ground. I lower the basket so that she can return the corn to where they belong. I picture Our Lady plucking Carlos and Hector from the soldiers and dropping them back into the safety of our village where they belong.

I toss each emptied cob into the bin, where it will lie until we use them on the fire to dry out this year's corn. We work in silence until there is no corn left. I join Abuela, who is pinching *masa*, forming the soft mush in the palms of her hand. We wrap each one in a piece of corn husk, tying the end with a thin strip of leaf string to keep the *masa* together in the pouch as it cooks.

"Come Tomasa," Mama says. We attach our looms to the ceiling beam and start to weave. Like Mama, I cannot sit without something for my hands to do. *Please bring them back*, I pray, as I work the thread through from left to right. *Bring them back to us*, my heart pleads, as I begin the thread from right to left.

Maria falls asleep in Abuela's arms. Once Manuelito has finished with the firewood, he sulks outside. I hear him murmuring to the goat while he tries to stay close to us. He and I would have helped Papa search for the boys if Papa had let us.

Mama strikes a match to light the lamp. The sun sets. The air chills. I look up through the doorway to see a large moon rising. My fingers keep the thread moving.

Bring them back. Please, bring them home.

I am surprised when suddenly I hear Manuelito run from the house. Mama and I jump up. Mama holds on to the entryway. My eyes take a moment to adjust to the darkness.

When I see them, I run. It does not take long before I see something is wrong. I slow down.

There is Papa. Manuelito has caught up with them. And there is no mistaking Carlos, who now carries Manuelito on his back.

But where is Hector? Surely he would have walked back with them.

When they reach me, I stretch out my hand to Carlos, who squeezes it, then releases it.

I go on searching the moonlit road until I am convinced it is empty. Then I turn and watch the men of my family as they reach the circle of light where Mama waits.

✿ ✿ ✿

After dinner, Papa or Abuela or Mama usually tell us a story from long ago, a fable or tale, they have learnt from their parents, like the one about the loud disobedient children who turned into monkeys, or the mice who hoped for a boy-child. Tonight, though, Papa tells us a new story – one he has never told before. He tells how he found an army truck that was gathering young men. His words have the sureness of a legend told over and over, passed down through the years, even though it happened only hours ago.

"I told the first soldier that I would go and get Carlos' papers to prove that he is only fourteen. But the soldier would not listen. So I spoke to the driver, who said he could not help. Then I went to the back of the truck."

He describes a truck like the one we saw on the way to market this morning. Papa said the back of the truck yawned open. Canvas covered the sides, so he could not see all the faces inside.

"I asked another soldier if he would check for my son, who must have been mistaken for someone older. That soldier called, 'Carlos!' Young men on the truck stood back and Hector and Carlos came out to where I could see them both," Papa says.

"'I don't want to feed all these worms,' the soldier told me. 'He's too skinny, anyway,' he said, pointing to Carlos. 'Take him home and fatten him up.'"

I held my breath.

"I asked them to let Hector off the truck too, but

another soldier moved between me and the soldier who had called the boys worms. 'Don't push your luck.' the soldier said."

"So Hector has gone with the soldiers," I say, when Papa will not. And I think: how will his mother survive without him to help in the fields? Who will keep the truck running? What will Catarina do without her beloved brother? And what about me? Would being a soldier change what is unspoken between Hector and me?

Papa stands up. "I will go to tell Doña Veronica and Catarina what has happened."

"I want to go with you," Carlos says.

Abuela interrupts. "Let me put this ointment on your feet, Carlos." I had not noticed, until then, the dried blood on both his heels.

"Veronica will need you tomorrow to help in their field with Hector away." Hector left school last year and has worked like a man ever since. That was when the bus to the city broke through the wooden slats of the bridge. Only a few passengers were pulled alive from the gorge. The father of Catarina and Hector was not one of them.

"I think it would be better if you rested," Papa says.

Carlos refuses the food Mama puts out for him.

Before I fall asleep, I hear Papa return. He and

Mama speak in hushed voices. I cannot understand what they are saying.

I know Hector would never be mean. If Hector is a soldier, then I will not believe that soldiers are as bad as some people think.

In my dream, the soap woman from the market asks Mama to do a design of soldiers marching on her next huipil. A large green truck roars through the market, scattering people's work. It stops and the back yawns open like the mouth of a monster. It transforms itself into a cave with a beast living inside, gobbling up anyone who tries to pass. Two soldiers drag Hector and Carlos towards the monster's mouth. The boys dig in their heels, trying to stop themselves being devoured. Four lines mark the dirt, swaying like snakes.

CHAPTER 3

This morning, Carlos hardly eats a thing before he leaves for Doña Veronica's fields. Manuelito and I wait outside for Catarina, so we can walk to school together.

"Mama is sure Hector will send us money from what the army pays him," Catarina tells me. Her eyelashes flutter nervously like butterfly wings. She blinked and blinked like this for months after the bus that her father was on crashed. "Hector might even be able to come home for my wedding," she says. And then, as if to build a wall against disappointment, she adds, "He might come if he finishes his training." Catarina blinks three more times before I turn away and look down at the path in front of my toes.

The village is awake. Voices greet each other. Manuelito and a friend race past us. I look up at smoke rising from the fire where Doña Michaela is boiling threads to dye them yellow. I feel the blue of the sky against the green mountain. I want to believe Hector will see this place again, run on to the soccer field during market, work his field and hear the corn grow. I want to believe that what Catarina says is true.

✿ ✿ ✿

Life weaves a new pattern. Each morning Carlos eats hardly anything, as though less food will stop him being transformed into the man that he tries to hold under his skin. He steps resolutely out to Doña Veronica's to work in her field.

As soon as we are done with school, Manuelito and I go to our field. As I help free our crops of weeds, I think of the patterns I could weave. I wonder what Hector will say when he sees plants growing, birds flying, clouds floating, and a football sitting just outside the goal. When he comes home for Catarina's wedding, I will show him what I have woven. After what has happened in the last few months, I do not want to think about the soldiers or guerrillas coming to recruit her sweetheart.

✿ ✿ ✿

Mama and I walk with our bundles on our heads. We come to the place where the stream parts the trees and meanders around boulders, the way a comb being pulled through my hair might be pushed off course by an insect bite.

Patches of sun shine on rocks in the stream. And in this spot where the tree canopy opens, we girls and women of the village laugh and talk as we wash clothes in the moving water. We lay them out on the rocks and over bushes and low branches. The sun lights up their splashes of colour and warms them, drinking the wetness from the green, red, blue, white and yellow threads.

Doña Rena's daughter leads her blind mother to the group of women. "Is that Catarina I hear?" Doña Rena asks, as she finds the edge of her stool with her fingertips. She eases herself down. Once settled, she sits there like a Mayan queen. She is older than even Abuela, who has not come to the stream since before Maria was born.

Doña Rena has a way of finding the soft spot in each of us and poking it with her words. Today it is Catarina's turn.

"I'm telling you this story as a favour," Doña Rena says.

"Lucky you," Catarina's mother says. Catarina flushes anxiously as the old woman talks about her wedding party long ago.

The story begins early in the week before Doña's wedding, when every preparation seemed to go wrong.

It doesn't take long for her to get to the day of the wedding:

"… So the pig strayed into the house when we were not looking and ate the entire bowl of *masa*. We had to start grinding corn all over again. Then the monkey took the entire basket of *tamales*… and after that, the women had to start cooking all over again before the dancing could start."

"Hey, you forgot the parrot this time," Doña's sister says.

The other women laugh.

Usually they bounce their teasing back and forth until someone throws in something new to push and pull across the stream. But Doña's story fascinates the younger ones. We are not old enough to have heard it told a hundred times already.

"And if you start your marriage with all that work, you have to go on working hard your whole life," Doña Rena warns us, "just like I have."

"Just like you have?" Doña Rena's sister asks, with her toothless grin. Everyone erupts in laughter. "No one here believes you, especially not a smart girl like Catarina," her sister says, shaking her head, "…especially the part about you working hard." She turns back to laying out her wash on a drying rock.

"Oh, how can you talk like that to your older sister?" Mama scolds, "especially when she has come

here just to encourage the rest of us while we work."
There is a ripple of laughter.

"Yes, I think I deserve your respect," says Doña
seriously, and the women laugh again.

The drone of the grower's plane drowns out the
music of our laughter. Our smiles flatten. The pilot
flies so low that the tips of the trees could scratch the
belly of his plane. Silence falls and darkens our mood.

"That plane spits poison," Mama says, as she dips
the fabric she holds in and out of the water. She rubs
salt on the wet skirt.

No one replies. No one nods or says, "Yes, this
is true, *es verdad*," as Mama turns the corner of the
cloth in on itself and scrubs one side against another.
Her words make all the women look down, even *Doña*
Rena, whose eyes cannot see.

"The day after that plane rained chemicals on to
the fields, some of the children vomited for days."
Mama goes on, as if they did not already know this,
as if they had not all been to the funeral of Doña's
granddaughter.

Mama dips the skirt into the stream again and
rubs it with salt in another stained place. The only
sound is the rush of splashing water over rocks. The
women's hands push and pull clothes in and out of
the stream, as if the force of their work could dissolve
Mama's lingering words.

The shiny metal plane and the truth Mama speaks have captured the laughter and flown it away.

One by one, the women finish their work. "Till tomorrow," Doña Michaela says, putting her bundle on to her head and turning to leave.

"Till then," Mama says, as we gather our things. I nod goodbye to Catarina, who is kneeling next to her mother.

With each step we take, the sound of the stream pulls away from Mama and me.

✿ ✿ ✿

Days pass, and I have almost forgotten the chill of the women's silence at the stream. We are lying on our sleeping mats and Papa begins the story of Toad and Vulture's short-lived friendship, when Vulture gives Toad a ride on his back. As Papa reaches the part where Vulture drops inconsiderate Toad, a truck without lights rumbles past our house.

Thud. Something hits the wall of our *ni'tzja*.

We follow Papa outside. The sliver of moon is not enough to show whose truck it was. Papa crouches down in front of a paper-covered bundle the size of a fist. He unties the string and flattens the paper on the ground, where the light from our doorway shines on it. There is a rock inside.

"What is it?" Abuela asks.

Carlos, who stands behind Papa and Mama leans back into the *ni'tzja*. "A letter," Carlos tells Abuela.

"What does it say?" Abuela asks.

Papa brings the letter inside, close to the light.

I tell her the words of the letter:

"STOP mAkInG tRouBle."

Each letter of "STOP" is thick and loud, cut from the big headline of a newspaper. "Making" and "trouble" speak like a mouthful of broken teeth, uneven and thinner.

"What trouble?" Manuelito asks.

"Don't worry, son," Mama said. "It is nothing." She folds up the paper and tucks it into the waist of her skirt, as though she knows the words belong to her.

CHAPTER 4

It is two weeks since the letter was thrown at our house. In church I pray: "Thank you, Blessed Mother, *Gracias Nuestra Madre*, for no more night-time visitors." Our priest is still away visiting other villages, so it is our catechist who has read the gospel and now blesses us. We emerge from the dark church into a soft rain. I wonder where Padre Luis will stay when he returns. While he was away, soldiers moved into his small room behind the church.

We follow the path home. Manuelito races to show Abuela the mushrooms he has found. She is sitting outside waiting for us. She said her legs felt too heavy for her to come to church with us this morning, so we said prayers for her, while she sat here praying for us.

"Beautiful!" she says, looking at what Manuelito has gathered. "The first of the season!" Then she turns to Carlos and me. "Go inside with your brother now."

I watch through the doorway as she passes a piece of paper to Mama, who opens it slowly. She and Papa look at the paper silently. I know they are trying to understand what it says.

"Carlos," Papa calls. From my spot of the floor, I can see Carlos softly reading the message to them. Mama's hands begin to tremble and the paper crinkles, as she folds it into a tiny bundle. Then she talks to Abuela in a voice too low for me to hear.

Mama does not show me this letter. Somehow I know that it has to do with her talking about the cloud sprayed on the fields that makes the children sick.

After we eat, I draw a *dibujo* of the plane flying over the fields, leaving a pale green cloud behind it.

✿ ✿ ✿

Tonight, I wake up from a dream of the jagged teeth – letters tearing at the wall of our ni'tzja, while I cough green. In the darkness, I wipe away the spit from the side of my mouth. I will check in the morning to be sure my fingers and mouth show no trace of green.

✿ ✿ ✿

Two days after the second letter, I awake to find Mama and Carlos gone. At first I think they must be outside, but Papa shakes his head to tell me not to look.

They have vanished into the night.

"Why did they leave us?" Manuelito asks. Before Papa can answer, Manuelito demands, "Why didn't they take me with them?" He has never been away from Mama before. None of us have.

"You are a smart boy," Papa says. "You want your Mama and brother to be safe. But they can travel faster if it's just the two of them."

"I am a fast runner." Manuelito says.

"That's true," Papa answers. He takes a deep breath and continues. "My son, they will return when things are better."

"Where did they go?" Manuelito wants to know. We all do.

"They have several places to go. It depends what they find on their journey. But, son" – he says this to all of us – "it's safer if we don't know where they are. If anyone asks, it's better we say that they are visiting my father in the city."

I look up to see that most of Abuela's plants, herbs,and roots are gone from the ceiling poles. I look in the corner and notice that only half our woven clothes are still there waiting for market.

"But they didn't wake us up to say goodbye," Manuelito cries. Papa picks him up and carries him to the field, where they will work side by side until long after his tears dry.

When Papa and Manuelito are gone, Abuela echoes what I am thinking. "Your Mama knows how to make medicine from the plants, which will help them stay well. And they can trade the remedies for food along the way."

Mama and Carlos have really gone. And yet Mama did not say goodbye to us, so I could not tell her to take care.

Abuela pulls me out of these sad thoughts. "And Tomasa, your Mama was proud to take your belts and *dibujos* with her."

I am not glad Mama had to go, but it makes me feel better to know that she has something with her that I have made. I hope my work brings money to help them on their journey. I know she does not need things in order to think of me, but as her hand touches what I have made, she will think of us sitting weaving, side by side, and I know she will smile.

After Papa and Manuelito come back and we have finished dinner, Papa tells the story about the wasps who conquered the jaguars. "Whoever said that a small creature must bow to the claws and teeth of the powerful jaguar?"

The picture I draw as he talks does not show a wasp with wings, or the black, sleek body of a jaguar. Instead, I draw a jagged black hole in the middle of our home and a father whose face has changed.

My dreams are as dark as the hole. Their heaviness wakes me. I lie there with my eyes closed. Then I remember, and reach out to the place where Mama should be sleeping. That part was not a bad dream.

Take care, Mama and Carlos, I pray. *K'awilawib.*

CHAPTER 5

"Go, go," Abuela says the next morning after we've eaten breakfast. "I am not completely useless yet." She turns to Manuelito, "On your way home, see what flowers and roots you can find."

I walk to the schoolhouse with Manuelito by my side. Maria rides on my back. She starts squirming, so I put her down. Even though she's holding my hand, she wobbles until she finds her balance. With Manuelito holding her hand on one side and me on the other, she walks unsteadily and we count her steps – almost thirteen before she asks to be picked up again.

At school, Maria watches us work. She has never been inside our classroom before, although I have played school with her at home, pretending she was my student. She listens to the teacher for a while, but then she grabs my arm and pulls herself up on her feet. Then she walks all by herself! The look of surprise on her face makes Catarina and some of the other children laugh.

Now Maria cannot keep still.

As I sit here, an idea wraps itself around me like a shawl. With Mama and Carlos gone, it would be better for my family if I stay at home and help Abuela. There would be one less fee to pay and I would have more time to weave and help to tie Abuela's herbs into bundles to sell at market. I could help her cook and sprinkle the floor with water.

At the end of the school day, I remind Manuelito about gathering plants for Abuela.

"I know!" he says, as though it is my fault Mama has left.

When Manuelito disappears outside, I wait for Señor Hernandez to finish speaking to another student. While I am waiting, I look at the books on his shelf.

"Look," I say to Maria, pulling down my favourite. It has photographs of deep blue water so wide that the shore is swallowed up. All that separates blue sea from sky is a thin blue line. I turn to a photograph of a pyramid surrounded by jungle, built by our Mayan ancestors. The next page shows three pyramids standing in a dry, sandy place. These were built by the ancestors of others who live across that blue water. How did their ancestors and mine think to build the same thing? I wonder if perhaps some of their ancestors crossed the water in boats and told the others.

I turn back to the Mayans. If one side did travel,

which side was it, the Egyptians or Mayans? Or did something inside their hearts travel that thin blue line across the ocean and inspire both peoples to build their pyramids?

I turn back to the Egyptian photograph. Maria touches the page. My finger draws the outline of each pyramid, the thin line separating sky from sand. Maria's movement echoes mine.

"Maria!" Señor Hernandez says as he re-enters the room. "It was nice to have you in school today." Maria hides her face in my shoulder.

"Tomasa," he turns to me. "Did you bring Carlos's work for me to check?"

Maria peeps out again as I speak. "No, Señor. Carlos is travelling with Mama to visit our grandfather in the city."

"Ah, I could have lent him a book for that long bus ride."

I do not answer. I wonder if he can read on my face or hear in my voice that I am lying?

"So will Maria be coming in Carlos's place?" Señor Hernandez says in a teasing way. Maybe he does know that their trip will be more than a visit. Maybe he knows that they have fled from the danger they were warned about in the letters. But if he does know this, I believe he would not tell the wrong people.

"I have to help my grandmother at home," I tell

him. But what I really want to ask him is: will he give me assignments the way he gave them to Carlos, when Carlos needed to work in the fields? Would Maestro do that for a girl?

Before I can gather my courage to ask, he says, "So will you have time to pick up your lessons, or should I send them home with Manuelito?"

When he says this, I cannot help but smile. "I will try to come to school when I can."

"If you can't, we will use our messenger. I'll look forward to you coming back to school when your family returns."

On our way home, I stop at church. Two candles are burning. I walk towards the altar. At the feet of the statue of San Jose, I kneel down. From the waist of my skirt I pull out a piece of yarn from the unfinished cloth Mama left on her loom.

"Please bring Mama back to finish the work she started," I say, and place the yarn across the saint's feet. "Send Mama back to us."

I take out Carlos's discarded medicine bundle that Abuela replaced with a fresh one before he left.

"And please keep Carlos safe," I ask the saint, as I lay the medicine bag on his other foot.

✿ ✿ ✿

Tonight, as Papa tells his story, I draw pyramids and work out a design to weave them into a belt. I pray that I will come to know some of the wisdom that grows inside us naturally, the wisdom we are meant to know.

"If you dropped a frog into water boiling on the *comal*, the frog would jump out and hop away," Papa says. "But if you scoop up a frog in a pot of water from the stream, it will grow used to the pot."

"Just as people become used to those model villages," Abuela says. The look on Papa's face asks her not to mention that place where guards force people to live between barbed wire away from their villages. Soldiers have emptied families out of their real villages and scattered them among different model villages in different parts of the country. So now all those people have to speak Spanish in order to understand each other. They have lost all their friends. Those model villages are full of suspicion and mistrust. I cannot imagine living in a place where you cannot walk down a road or to your field without permission from someone else.

Papa's voice pulls me back from my thoughts.

"If you were to carry the pot without sloshing the frog too much," he continues, "and then put it on the *comal*, you could light the small sticks under the flat metal on which the pot rests. You could then add bigger and bigger sticks to slowly heat the water.

"In the pot, the frog would become accustomed to the heat bit by bit, until the water got so hot that the frog would sink down dead in the water."

Papa looks at me as he finishes this story. I realise that the rumours we heard about the model villages are like the frog being scooped up into the pot. We get used to hearing about them, but we don't think they pose a danger to us. The soldiers arriving became the fuel to feed the fire. The letters were like the larger sticks. As much as I miss them, Mama and Carlos were right to leave – I have no doubt any more.

That night, on my mat, I dream I am standing in a huge pot. Water is being ladled in on top of me, rolling down my body, getting higher and higher in the pot until it reaches my chin. At first, I shiver in the cool water and I am grateful when I smell the fire and feel my feet start to warm.

I am startled to hear Papa's distant voice: "Tomasa, danger sneaks up slowly."

Danger? The warmth moving up towards my knees starts to feel uncomfortable. I hold my breath and crouch under water, then push off the bottom with all my might and reach for the edge of the pot. My fingers slide off – I can't quite reach. I suck in my breath, crouch down underwater and try again. My fingers grasp, but cannot hold the rim. I slip back into the pot. The ladle adds water again. Now the water is deep enough for me to float to the rim. I hoist myself over. Thud. I drop to the ground.

I wake up damp and shivering.

CHAPTER 6

Each morning, I cook the *tortillas* Abuela pats flat. Manuelito leaves for school. I sweep and sprinkle the floor and help Abuela prepare the beans and *tortillas* or *tamales* for later. Maria seems content with Abuela, but she cries more easily. Even though she cannot tell us, she must feel Mama and Carlos's absence just as the rest of us do. But the rest of us, who can use words to talk about the emptiness, do not speak of it.

As I return from washing clothes with the village women at the stream, Abuela asks, "Did anyone say anything while you were working?"

"Doña Michaela did well at market," I tell her.

"What else?" she asks.

Should I mention that some of the women touched my shoulder as they passed, but no one asked about Mama and Carlos? It was as if Mama had never knelt among them at the water, as if she and Carlos never existed. I cannot stop wondering which one of the women could have spoken within earshot of whoever wrote the letters. Or was the person who wrote the letters someone we know?

My head swims with questions, but I ask Abuela just one thing: "Do you think they know about the letters?"

"Are you asking because they didn't want to know why you were there alone? They knew about the letters, just as they know what you sold at market this week. They keep their distance from us and, I'm sure, from Hector's mother."

"Doña Veronica never looks at me now," I tell Abuela.

Abuela seems to read my mind. "One of those women wagged her tongue. Someone passed on what your mama said at the stream, about the grower's plane spitting poison. And either that person, or someone she talked to, told someone in the civil patrol. And the civil patrol told the soldiers."

"But the women would never try to hurt us," I say.

"In some villages there are altars where people pray the wrong things." Abuela says. "Maybe the men who work for the growers prayed the wrong things for us and that was why the trouble came."

"Why would they pray for things that would break up our family?"

"Tomasa, they'd do anything to move us all

away from this place just so that the grower could use all the land."

As Papa walks in, our words are stirred into the soup. We swallow them at dinner and speak of it no more.

✿ ✿ ✿

Days later, in the middle of the night, the next *amenaza* wrapped around a rock is thrown through our doorway.

Papa jumps up. I light the lamp.

"Go back to your mat," Papa tells me.

I lie down and open my eyes a slit. A sliver of light flows into them like a new moon. It is enough to see Papa. He looks at the paper. The lamp glows in front of him, between us, so I cannot see the number of words. He is struggling with the meaning of the message I know he cannot read. I could read it to him, but he does not ask me to.

In the morning, I wake thick with dreams that refuse to come to mind. But the dreams did not bring me the vision of Mama and Carlos that I prayed for.

✿ ✿ ✿

"Manuelito, I need you to help me in the field today," Papa says over breakfast, "We will go and talk to Maestro when he has finished teaching."

"I can tell him for you," I offer. Then I will be able to give in my assignment and get instructions for the next one.

"I'll do it," Papa says. His tone tells me he will tolerate no more discussion about who goes.

"Will you take this to him, then," I say. I pull the paper from under my folded sleeping mat. Papa looks down at my writing. "My work," I tell him. "For Señor Hernandez."

Manuelito looks back at me as he follows Papa out of the door. I wonder if he would rather be with his friends at school than working all day in the field.

I wonder what else Papa is going to talk over with Señor Hernandez.

✿ ✿ ✿

Morning begins a new row of chores. I am turning a *tortilla* over on the *comal* when I hear Manuelito cry out from the goat's pen. We all follow the sound. The goat has gone. A dark patch stains the dirt. Papa kneels down and pinches the discoloured ground. He lifts his fingers to his nose.

A green army pick-up truck slows down and pulls

in close to the pen. A soldier opens his door and walks towards the pen.

"What have we here?" he says.

"Our goat has gone," Manuelito blurts out.

The soldier squats down next to Papa and twists a finger into the moist earth. He tastes his finger.

"Blood," he says. "The guerrillas must have slaughtered your goat. They like to come at night and steal."

"We didn't see anyone," Manuelito says.

The soldier calls back to the truck. "Guerrillas have been here, just as we thought." He looks back at Papa. "Isn't that true?"

Papa will not say something that is not true, so he stays silent.

✿ ✿ ✿

The hope that things will get better evaporates. Papa does not say, and Abuela and I never admit that we believe Mama and Carlos will have to stay away longer than any of us thought.

Papa continues to keep Manuelito home from school. We all stay close to the house, yet we can see there are more soldiers driving past. Some arrive in our village in helicopters. There is no way we could ignore the *thwap, thwap, thwap* of their coming and going.

We hear the big machine they brought. And then we see it. On the outskirts of our village this thing with a big blade at the front has dug a long trench.

Gracias, Our Lady, I pray for the small happiness of spending time at market with Catarina today. I lay down a shawl. In the centre, I place weavings and small *dibujos* of flowers and fruit, *dibujos* of scenes from outside our house. None of the drawings hold the machines that fly above us or crawl past us on the road. I doubt anyone but the soldiers would want to buy those drawings.

Most of Mama's left-behind weavings have been sold, but there is one *huipil* that the soap woman admired last market. I know Papa will be pleased with the money I will bring home.

As I reach across to pull the far corner of the fabric to tie my bundle, Papa enters the house and breaks my happiness like a clay pot dropped on a rock.

"Put that away," Papa says.

"But it is Saturday," I tell him. He must be confused about the day of the week because we do not go to school any more.

"No market today," Papa replies.

"Yes. This is the market before *fiesta*." I am sure Papa must have forgotten, because these markets always produce the most sales.

"You will not go today," he says.

"But I will not be on the road alone," I say. "I travel with Doña Veronica."

"Not today," Papa says, and I know now to hold any further words.

My disappointment mixes with confusion. Could it be he does not want me to go because we cannot repay her for the ride with goat's milk?

Beep beep. Outside, Doña stops. As I move through the door towards the road, Catarina calls to me and jumps out the minute the truck stops. She hugs me. Papa has followed me outside and approaches the driver's side. I miss what Papa says as Catarina tells me about her fiesta preparations.

In the slight pause, as she waits for me to answer, I hear Doña say, "OK then," in a voice that reveals relief. "Come on, Catarina," she calls to her daughter. "Get back in. I do not want to be late."

"You are not coming?" Catarina asks.

All I can do is shake my head no.

"Hurry now, Catarina! I do not want to risk losing my place." Doña's voice holds a shrillness I have never heard before.

As she climbs back into the truck, Catarina looks at me as if I could answer her questions with my eyes. Doña pulls away before Catarina has closed the door. She is in such a hurry that the tyres kick up pebbles which hit my ankles and feet.

✿✿✿

As we leave church on Sunday morning, soldiers wait for us in the square. Some are standing in the open spaces between the houses. A light-skinned *ladino* with bars of colour on his uniform above his pocket stands in the back of an open truck. He is puffed up like a rooster. He watches us with distaste. Other soldiers herd us towards him. When we all are all standing in front of him, he reads aloud from a letter.

"Because of all the trouble in this village, there will be no more money for a teacher." Then he warns us not to have anything to do with guerrillas who may try to steal from us at night.

"And you must carry your identification card whenever you leave your homes. When you are gathering wood, you may be asked to show it. Each time you leave for your fields, have it ready."

Clouds move over the sun as the villagers unravel to return home. Some of them are whispering about model villages. What would Mama and Carlos do if they returned and we were not here? How would they know where to find us?

When we get home, Manuelito tells Abuela what the soldier said.

"*Ay,*" Abuela says. "Nothing was stolen from us until the soldiers came."

"No more of that," Papa says in a dark voice that frightens me.

As we sit down to eat, Maestro calls from outside. Papa welcomes him in and Abuela signals me to offer him food.

"No, no, thank you. I have only come to say goodbye," he says. "I hope this trouble will end soon. And then, who knows? The village might invite me back." Then he says, "But even if they choose a new teacher, I want you to know what a great pleasure it has been to have known you all." He bows towards Abuela, and then ruffles Manuelito's hair.

"I'm getting a lift into town, so I must hurry. I wonder if Tomasa and Manuelito could go to the school and pick up the books I could not fit into my boxes. Would you keep them for me?"

"Of course," Papa says.

"Could they go now?" Maestro asks.

"Of course."

If Maestro is leaving, I want to wait with him until he leaves. I don't want to miss anything. When we hesitate, Abuela shoos us out.

Manuelito and I both hug Maestro. Reluctantly I follow Manuelito to the school.

I hear a jeep behind us. Soldiers. My heart jumps: we have not brought our identity cards with us.

What if they stop? What will I tell them?

The jeep slows down. I grab Manuelito's hand.

Keep driving, I pray.

The jeep's motor sputters and stops.

"Not again!" a soldier cries out to the driver. "Where did you learn to drive?"

Manuelito and I keep walking. I keep praying: *Keep us invisible.*

"These roads are nothing but ruts," one says, before the engine roars again.

They pass us without stopping.

Gracias, Our Lady.

We duck into the school. On the shelf are four books. One has bright pictures of the alphabet that Maria will love. One has the flowers of Central America that Manuelito has looked at so often, he has worn the cover thin. The other book about our Mayan ancestors is for Carlos. I smile at Maestro for believing that Carlos will return. The last book has photographs of the pyramids. I know this one is for me. There is nothing else left of Maestro but two boxes stacked by the door.

I dash home ahead of Manuelito. My heart smiles when I see Maestro is still there. But I wish my ears could not hear what he is telling Papa and Abuela.

"...Recruiting boys as young as ten," he is saying.

Manuelito rushes through the door behind me

and throws himself into Maestro's arms. I watch Manuelito's cheeks, half-moons sitting on either side of his nose below dark eyes that sparkle like water in a stream when the sun catches it. How would his face change if the army took him? I dare not think of Hector.

I notice Papa fold a paper and slip it under his belt as Maestro says, "Adios."

I hope Abuela will tell me what they have been talking about tomorrow, when Papa and Manuelito go to the field before the fiesta.

Doña Veronica's truck stops to pick up Maestro. "See you at the fiesta tomorrow!" Catarina calls to me. I smile at the prospect of sharing secrets with her.

"I am grateful to you," Papa says to Maestro, as they shake hands through the open window.

Maestro pats his hand on the door of the cab and the truck moves off.

CHAPTER 7

As the rest of the village busies itself preparing for the fiesta, I discover that Papa has begun preparations of a different kind.

"We're going on a trip," Papa says. When he explains, Manuelito blurts out, "I don't want to leave." What he means is, he does not want to follow Mama and Carlos. Where once he hated them for leaving him behind, now he cannot imagine leaving to find them. There is only one way Mama and Carlos could make amends for deserting him and that is by coming back here.

"We'll arrive in Guatemala City in time to see the road to the cathedral painted with coloured sawdust and flowers," says Papa. "Manuelito, you won't believe how many kinds of flowers they have in the city at Easter to keep the saints from touching the ground. They are all placed just so, with bright sawdust just like the sawdust we use. And the designs! You can't imagine. We will have to buy Tomasa paper so she can sketch them. We will watch the whole procession, my son. Then you can decide if we should walk behind it and pick up some of the flowers."

Tempting as it all sounds, Manuelito is still thinking of Mama and Carlos. "Why don't they come back to us?"

Papa pretends not to hear. I watch as my father packs the few things we can't take with us that might tempt any soldiers who come by. He adds the books and a statue of Our Lady of Guadalupe to the cloth bundle and wraps it again in oilcloth, which he secures with a thin rope. Then he takes Manuelito off with him to bury the bundle as the sun falls asleep.

A silence hovers between Abuela and me. My stomach curls as I steal a glance at my grandmother. How will she be able to travel to the city if her legs will not take her as far as the stream or even to church? I have to know. But how do I ask such a thing?

"Abuela..."

Abuela looks into my eyes. She takes a deep breath. Then, nodding her head, she smiles. "Thank you for not asking when Manuelito was here. You are a smart one, Tomasa. Come now, help me get things ready for your trip."

She pulls out her clay-baked jar of herbs and unwraps each square of fabric, pulling out half of each of the roots, leaves, stems and dried flowers.

She points to some plants hanging from the rafters. She tells me about each of them – whether I need just the leaves, or if I should break off the branch or only the dried blooms from the end of the stem. Some I know, others I don't. As we place each into a new square of fabric, she tells me what it's for. "This will stop a fever." "Make this one into a tea for diarrhea." Thank the Virgin that Manuelito knows some of this, because I could never remember it all!

"I cannot give you all of them because you are taking my gatherer with you."

The thought of Abuela being here alone makes me shudder.

When we have finished, the questions tear at my heart.

How can we leave her behind?

How could she travel with us on the steep slope of the mountains?

"What about Doña Veronica?" I ask. "Couldn't she take you to the bus as she took Maestro?"

"That woman does not need more troubles than she has already. Let me stay here where I was born." Maria crawls into her lap. "We would only slow you down."

Oh. Maria too? I did not think we would leave Maria behind.

I lean against Abuela. Her arm reaches around

my shoulder. She holds me as I start to cry. When Maria starts crying too, Abuela takes her arm from me. "We will be waiting here for all of you to return."

"But Abuela..." I begin.

"Enough. Doña Nosey will send her daughter to check on the house when she sees you aren't at the stream. They will not let us starve. Our village wouldn't do that. We will be fine here until you come home again. Now, dry your tears."

Our talk is knotted into Abuela's bundle when Papa and Manuelito return from burying our treasures. Manuelito's knees are caked with dirt.

"Time for a story," Papa says. Abuela takes Manuelito and then me in turn and ties a new medicine pouch around our necks. She blesses us with words and the sign of the cross, with a smile and a kiss on our foreheads.

When we are settled, Papa begins.

"The vulture and the hawk were so hungry. As they flew, they were overjoyed to see a bag-of-bones horse lying in a field. With growling stomachs, they circled the carcass. Their hunger cried out for a meal," With eyes closed, Maria sighs, as if she dreams of the hunger of which Papa speaks.

Papa pauses. "But the vulture let his desire for that meal cloud his judgment. The hawk continued to circle, not sure whether the horse was alive or dead.

But the vulture saw only what he wanted to see – a meal.

"And when the vulture landed and stabbed at the flesh of the horse, the horse reared up and trampled on the vulture. So the cautious hawk lived, while his friend the careless vulture died."

"We should be cautious and stay here," Manuelito says with enough force to wake Maria. She grizzles, until I settle down next to her.

"The troubles have not died down yet," Papa answers softly.

I know this will not be like our games of statues, where we are out as soon as someone sees us move, but then we get another turn. If we are caught at this game, there is no next time.

I whisper to Maria, "What a wonderful time we're going to have." I move the tiny medicine pouch that has shifted to my shoulder back over my heart. "And afterwards, we will return." I hope that saying those words will help me believe them. I pray to believe.

In my dream, I am opening all the small bundles. Which one do I use for a poultice to lay on a wheezing chest? I cannot remember, as I listen to Abuela's laboured breathing.

In my strange dream city I call, "Manuelito!" but he is lost in the crowd in front of the cathedral. Abuela lies on the colourful carpet of sawdust and red, white, pink and purple flowers struggling for breath. I smooth back her hair as the procession of people steps over her. I taste the blue, the orange and yellow flowers.

"Abuela!" I shout, as I turn to see a giant owl fly off with Maria in its talons.

I wake myself up and feel Abuela's hand on my back. I turn to her.

She holds me in her arms until Papa signals that it is time to go.

CHAPTER 8

I tame my tears as I braid my hair. Mama would not cry, so I won't either.

Papa gently scoops up Manuelito and gives him to Abuela. Then he rolls all our sleeping mats together.

"Save your energy for the journey," Mama would say if she were here. My fingers brush the string hammock that I'm leaving behind. It was the last thing I wove sitting next to Mama. "We'll need to sleep on the ground so we can't be seen," Papa told us last night. And so the hammock will be left behind in Abuela's care.

I wrap my skirt around my waist. I cannot see the red, yellow, and white corn on a blue background. I feel for the three patches. One lies over a hole I ripped in the fabric with a nail. The second patch hides our money. The third, our identification cards that Abuela has hidden well with tiny stitches. She told me that it will be better to pretend we are from wherever we are found, rather than let the identification cards say we are from a place where the soldiers have been.

I pull my *huipil* over my head and reach each arm through it. I touch the threads I embroidered, recognise them even in the dark. Each *quetzal* wears a shadow, an extra line that makes it look as though it has a third and fourth feather in its tail – as though it is better equipped to survive if a trapper tries to steal a feather. It would be nice to feel you had something extra, so that if a feather was plucked from you, you would still have enough feathers left to fly with.

I pack the small bundle Abuela has prepared for me and add a change of clothes and *tamales*.

I leave behind a *dibujo* for Catarina. In the picture, my doll sits on the shelf where I will leave the drawing. Abuela will know to give the picture to Catarina, and Catarina will know the message in my heart. I leave a second drawing of Mama, Papa, my brother, and me for Abuela and Maria. How I will miss them!

Papa checks on me. I nod to him and he nods back in the faint light of the moon that spills in through the window.

Maria wakes as I kiss her goodbye. She smiles at my finger in front of my lips. She stays quiet and looks hard at my face. I try to smile back, the way Mama and Abuela would.

Papa lifts sleeping Manuelito from Abuela's arms, putting his strong fingers gently on Manuelito's lips when my brother starts to talk. I arrange the fabric on my head and secure my bundle there. We do this silently, with only the moon watching. We do not want to wake Abuela from her pretend-sleep. If she can say that she did not see us leave, that she does not know where we have gone, they cannot make her tell what she does not know. She rolls over on to her side with her face to the wall, her arm around Maria.

As sure as the sun rises tomorrow, the men in the civilian patrol will tell the soldiers we have left. Those men will say our names and point towards our house when they meet the soldiers in the room behind the church. But if we stay, it will be only a matter of days before the danger from the threatening letters that follows us like a snake will strike.

I take one deep breath before we move through the door.

On the path, I see the figure a second before Papa does. I stop behind him.

"It's a bit early to be going to the fiesta." The soldier's voice makes me shudder.

"There is enough moonlight to work in the field before fiesta," Papa says.

"Why are you taking all those bundles?" I can barely make out the soldier's city accent, but the cold in his voice chills me.

"These are offerings for our altar up on the

mountain," Papa responds.

"Keeping the old Mayan ways is not a good idea. And if those things you are carrying are for the guerrillas, it will be the worse for you." This soldier is not alone. I see another farther down the path.

"Thank you for your advice…" Papa says.

"You'll be missed at the fiesta if you stay too long in your field or at your altar. You'd better take your children back into your *casita* now."

The soldier turns and walks towards the other, who moves closer to our house.

"Watch them," he says.

We retreat into our house.

Abuela has heard everything. She puts out her arms to me and rocks me as if I am a baby, while Maria curls up and falls asleep again. Manuelito and Papa lie on their mats, but I can tell by his breath that Papa can't sleep either.

✿ ✿ ✿

As the church bell rings, we reach the village square, careful not to disturb the sawdust design that paints the path in front of the church. As we settle inside, I pray that we may escape as Papa has planned. I pray also that the soldiers who kneel down with us during Mass cannot hear my prayers.

Padre Luis offers the final blessing. Papa helps the men gather all the small offerings that have been left at San Jose's feet, along with Mama's piece of yarn and Carlos' medicine pouch. Three of the men gently lift the statue from its place on the altar. They turn to place him on the waiting platform. Four men hold the handles jutting out from the sides of the platform waist high. Once the offerings return to their place at his feet, one of the men says "Now!" As one, they lift the handles up on to their shoulders to walk our saint outside.

We step into the stream of neighbours and become part of the procession as we follow the statue that floats above the crowd.

One of the soldiers stares. Three leave the square. Others lean against the church. Two sit on the tailgate of a truck and smoke, talking between themselves. They are blind to our song, although our shadows touch them as we march by.

Only once a year on his feast day does our saint have the chance to breath fresh air and feel the sun and breeze on his face. I imagine he is heavy with all the pain that has been placed at his feet. The things we ask of him weigh him down. He carries the burdens with him now as our voices sing him around the plaza.

When the procession winds him back towards the church, Padre Luis prays with us again outside the church doors. He prays for peace, for understanding, for the souls of our departed. The people do not look up, but I feel them tense when Padre prays for the soldiers, some of whom still stand watching us.

Before the saint is returned, two men take the burdens from him so that he can enter the church wiped clean and relieved of our prayers. Each offering, like the medicine bag from Carlos and the string from Mama's loom, are taken to a prepared pile of wood. Each is placed in a different niche, then a match is struck. It is held first to one place and then to another. The flames lick and devour our offerings. Smoke takes them skyward to Our Lady and God.

❁ ❁ ❁

The fiesta's sights and sounds surround me. People seem more precious when I know that soon I will miss them. When my happiness is interrupted by a worry that Manuelito might mention our leaving to his friends, I pray to Our Lady, that I may enjoy this afternoon.

We eat and visit people and dance. The young ones play football and the day rushes on. The sun sets and torches are lit. Like a bird preening, my village seems puffed up and bigger than itself.

Ba boom! My heart jumps. I look up from the

village square expecting to see fireworks explode and paint colour on the sky. But the sky is dark.

Another loud *boom* silences the round sound of the *marimba*. Voices fade, laughter falls, and dancers pause. A third explosion cracks the air. A firm push on my shoulder from an elder tells me all I need to know. I pull Maria to the earth with me.

Villagers extinguish the torches. I hear a baby's cry erupt on the tail of the next *boom* that is followed by hundreds of small, quick pops. The baby's cry is muffled, then stops. He must have been put to his mother's breast.

But the sound of shots continues, echoing across the top of the trees, over the houses and church. No one moves. It is as if we have melted into the ground. I whisper, *"Alto Señorita Hummingbird"* in Maria's ear and force a smile. I try to slow my heart by thinking about the colours of the fiesta, bright as ripe mangoes and papayas ready for picking.

I do not want to think about what is happening in the next village as the small pops continue. The smell of food left to burn on a nearby *comal* stings my nose.

As the minutes pass and the shots die down, Maria falls asleep. I keep my arm under her neck but turn on to my back so that I lie flat against the earth.

Looking up at the sky, I try to ignore the glow

coming from the direction of the noise. But I cannot.

I want Abuela to explain what is happening. Later, when we stop to say one more goodbye and gather our bundles and leave Maria, I will ask her.

My arm under Maria's head is numb. My body feels stiff and hard like wood. I try to think myself flexible like tall corn in the breeze. I plan what I would weave tomorrow if I weren't going away. Then I think how I would weave a design of vine tendrils that grow up the *ceiba* tree. I would add the giant tear shape of the grey nest that the noisy *Montezuma* builds.

I will think about a *quetzal*'s long, green, curved tail feathers hanging from a low branch, tickling Maria's nose. Maybe that will make Manuelito smile again.

Everything is silent now, but tight as the knots in the cloth on Mama's loom.

CHAPTER 9

The glow in the sky fades. The quiet in our village relaxes like a taut thread which has been cut.

Mama and Carlos would have liked the fiesta. Well, Mama would have. I draw a picture in my mind of the two women I saw who wore *huipil*es from Mama's loom.

Carlos would have been lost without *compañeros*. The boys his age have almost all gone. There aren't many young men for the girls to glance at and few to notice them. Tonight's dancing has to go on without those who have been forced into the army, spirited away to fight with the guerrillas, or who have fled north to escape, or just gone – disappeared.

No, Carlos would have been sad at today's fiesta. He would have noticed the empty eyes of the one boy who was brought back, heard stories of the jumble of bones never returned. Today would have made Carlos think of Hector.

And neither Mama nor Carlos would have liked

the way some people in our village look away when they see us. Some people are friendly, but some do not want us here any more. They think they might catch trouble from us. That it might rub off on to them like pollen from flowers. That the trouble we carry might spill on to the ground where they might step in it and take it home on their feet. They do not want trouble in their *ni'tzja*.

What if someone went to one of those altars Abuela told me about and prayed the wrong things about our village?

No. I will think about the good things here today – the feel and taste of the chicken and pig on this feast day. But even with these treats, nothing tastes as warm as *tayuyo* — the *masa* and black beans wrapped in leaves made from the corn and beans we grow in our field. It is Mama's favourite, too.

Mama. I start to shake as I picture the letters cut out and glued on to the paper. This horror of glowing skies is no longer just a whisper that passes from mouth to mouth, from village to village. I try to quieten myself with thoughts of a blanket whose design I weave on to my heart. I will think about the delicious meal we have just eaten and weave memories into the blanket, so I can lie under them and never forget that full feeling of fiesta. I will think a time when we will come back home and plant our corn again in rows of seven:

four for the family, one for the thief, one for the birds and one for the wind.

As a village elder touches my shoulder, a sob from deep down inside shakes me once and escapes in relief. In the darkness, I watch the elders go from one person to the next. We stir. We stretch as if the elders hold magic to bring us all back to life. I pray for a thin blue line to connect us to the village that glowed tonight, so that the people there will get up as we do.

The *marimba* begins, sounding soft, like water in the stream.

I stand up and reach down to retrieve my sleeping sister. Papa comes across the plaza with Manuelito shuffling by his side. I reach for my brother's hand as we turn to walk along the dirt path to our field. But he pulls away.

I want to scream at him, "It is not Mama's fault!" But I do not speak. I am left only to my silent prayers of safe journey and forgiveness. We walk through the silence that surrounds the uneasiness dividing our family, as well as what stands before us in the dark.

✧✧✧

At home, we hug Abuela and Maria one last time.

"Later," I tell my sister. Our goodbye is quick. We extinguish the lamp. Papa, Manuelito and I wait a moment to let our eyes adjust to the dark. We move into the corn. When we are already through our field and into the trees, we hear a helicopter come closer and hover over our village. We hear shots and an explosion. When the first thread of smoke finds us, the smell stings and seeps inside to cloud my brain and jumble my thoughts. I put my bundle down. Without saying a word to Papa or Manuelito, I turn back and run, leaving them both behind. I feel as though a fist has grabbed my heart and is plucking it from my chest. I do not think about the soldiers finding me. I run back to where voices call out for help, for mercy. As I approach the north end of the village, my lungs feel empty.

I pray myself invisible as I move along the edge of the trees. My eyes go from one thing to the next, unable to understand the still bundles lying on the ground shadowed by flames that eat at the church and the houses on either side.

I race until I am close enough to see our house is not yet lit. I run towards it. I move as if I am invisible through the open place. Inside, I find the shelves and the things on them broken and scattered on the floor. The book, the doll, Abuela's herb pot, her sleeping mat and her loom are scattered. The picture is crumpled

"Abuela? Maria?"

And when I see they are not here, I pray *Gracias,*

Nuestra Madre. They got away!

I leave the house, slip around the side.

"Abuela," I whisper into the darkness.

I hear footsteps on the path and see light approaching. I slip behind the *ni'tzja*, out of view of the soldier coming with a torch. When I hear him call out, I want to scream, *You are too late. This family has escaped you.*

He throws his torch on to the thatched roof. As the blaze takes hold, I move along the far side and when I see the soldier's back, I run across the open space towards the field. As I enter the undergrowth, I trip and fall over a still bundle.

I have fallen over Abuela.

I hold her now, between the rows of corn where she sought safety. I rock her in small motions so that I will not rock the stalks that shelter us.

I barely feel the hand on my shoulder.

"Tomasa," Papa says, in a way that tells me he is thankful he has found me. Maria is in his arms. He reaches down and holds on to Abuela's neck, then closes her eyes with the palm of his hand.

I search Abuela's face for some signal, some small sign. And then I realise that she has left us. I hold her tightly and hide my face in her hair, the way Maria does to me when she's frightened.

"Tomasa," Papa whispers again.

I breathe in Abuela's smell. How can I let her go?

"Tomasa, we have to leave."

How can I leave her?

"Manuelito is waiting in the forest," Papa says gently. Maria starts to grizzle.

Papa gently pulls on my arm. I let Abuela go. My body shakes so hard that at first I cannot move my feet. He holds me. I cover my face with my hands, as though that could wipe out the things I have just seen.

A noise makes my heart skip. Movement.

Papa pulls me farther down the row, deeper into the shadows. The sound comes again. My breath is shallow. We wait and listen and hope.

Cries from the village square carry broken notes, gravelly shouts. They are fewer and fainter. I hear the roof of our house crumble.

Papa moves deeper into the field. I follow. We walk from row to row before Papa stops. Maria starts to grizzle again, but even with that, I hear the other noise too. Someone is close. Is it someone from the village who needs help? Or is it a soldier looking for villagers who have escaped? Papa shushes Maria. We play statues again. When we move, the sound moves with us.

Papa grabs my arm and begins to run. The footsteps follow fast. Whoever it is, they are not hurt. Their footsteps feel closer. They begin to gain ground.

When the hand grabs my shoulder from behind, I cannot hold back the cry that freezes us all. The hand jerks me around. My legs tremble and I crumple to the ground. I looked at his shiny boots splattered with red mud, the dull green of his trousers.

Papa reaches out from the darkness and puts a hand on my back. He pulls me back to my feet and thrusts Maria into my arms. Then he moves in front of us.

We all stand as though someone had cried *"Alto!"* and we are frozen to this place.

"You are one of us," Papa says to the soldier.

My eyes move up from the soldier's feet, up past his slender waist, up past the rifle that hangs across his torso from his slight shoulders, up to the face that is not much higher than my own, a face that does not yet know a moustache. And when I take it all in, I know he is one of us.

We stand facing this Mayan boy who looks so much like Hector. He draws his rifle up to his shoulder. Papa tries to push me behind him, but I stay at his side.

"Back to the village," the soldier tells us, in a deeper voice than Hector's but one that says he did not grow up far from here. His gun shakes as it points at Papa's chest. A shout from the village startles him and I'm afraid he might shoot.

I move, so that he can see me in the moonlight. He must have a sister somewhere who would be dressed as I am. Maybe, as he sees me, he will remember her gentle teasing. Surely laughter must have followed him in his childhood, as it followed all of us before the trouble started.

"Let's get away from this place," Papa says.

"Back to the village," the boy says again, motioning with the end of the gun, as though these words are all he knows.

"The village is gone," Papa tells him.

This boy soldier says nothing, his eyes glassy like the old men of the village who have drunk too much at the fiesta. The gun now points at Papa's waist. The sound of a cricket cuts the air.

"We are just poor farmers," Papa says. "We can't do you any harm." The gun now points at Papa's knees.

Another shout from the edge of the field startles us all. The boy points the rifle towards Papa's chest. A soldier shouts again, asking if everything is OK.

Our soldier looks at Papa's chest. I think smoke has entered this boy and clouded his thinking. He might pull the trigger and kill my father. I move farther to the side so that he has to look at Maria and me.

The other soldier shouts again. "Don't worry

about the stragglers. The helicopter is on the way. Come quickly, or the machine guns will catch you."

The boy has beads of sweat across the bridge of his nose. He shouts back, sounding stronger than he looks, "Coming!"

Will he turn us in? Will he shoot us? What will happen to Manuelito if he does?

But the soldier does not do any of these things. He raises his gun, makes it ready. He shoots into the air.

Maria starts crying, as the soldier turns and stumbles back towards the village. Papa takes her from my arms. We run as quickly as we can. Maria stops crying. The *thwapping* of the helicopter gets louder and louder.

We run, then cut across rows of corn until we reach the edge of the field. The light of the moon cannot find us once we slip into the cover of the trees. I let out my breath slowly, silently.

We hear a spatter of gunshots, then the helicopter pulls away. I turn for a last look at our field as dawn lightens the shadows. Green stretches below us. The machine that dug the trench at the edge of the village is now crushing our cornfield.

We turn up into the mountain where Manuelito waits. Deep into the cover of the trees we slow down. Papa stops and turns. He moves a few steps back in the direction we have just come from. We must be close to where Manuelito waits. Papa turns and comes back slowly. He hands Maria to me and moves along the path. Motioning for me to stay, he disappears into the thick brush. He moves so silently that when he re-emerges farther along the path, I jump.

I expect to see Manuelito behind him, but he is on his own.

"He was here," Papa says.

We stand on the path, turning around and away from each other, our eyes searching, trying to sense where he might have gone.

When I see the movement ahead, I whisper, "Papa."

Manuelito runs at me and slaps at my hip. "Why did you run away?" He spits out these words with all the anger he feels for Mama and Carlos.

CHAPTER 10

As we walk, I tuck my feelings into my heart. I hide them away just as Papa tucked our small treasures into the oilcloth and hid them in the earth for when we return. Papa does not tell Manuelito about Abuela or about the human bundles lying in the village. I understand. I will not talk of them either.

Like the deer and monkeys, the parrots and toucans, we know to stay still and silent when the puma stalks. I will tuck everything else away, wrap memories with hope, bury them until later, when it will be safe. We slip quickly through the trees, pulled along by the strength of Mama's love reaching out to us. We need to move more swiftly than the snake.

✿ ✿ ✿

The day blurs. When we finally stop for the night, Papa tells us to sleep so that our feet point in the direction we will travel in when we wake. He says that will keep us from getting lost.

Manuelito asks for his favourite story. I long for something familiar to calm us before we try to sleep. Among the trees, Papa's words find my ears and for a few minutes I am at home with my family surrounding me.

"The *quetzal* was a plain green bird which once blended into the leaves of the jungle," Papa says, "until a conquistador came along on a horse and started threatening the people."

"He wanted our land," Manuelito says.

"Yes, son, *es verdad*. What you say is true… And our people had never seen a horse before. The Mayan king was brave and did battle with this strange man with four legs and two heads." I draw this image in the dirt with my finger as the story unfolds.

"The king fought fearlessly. He stabbed the horse, thinking the conquistador and the horse were one." Manuelito pokes his finger into the chest of the horse I've drawn.

"Ah," Manuelito says, and falls over on his side.

I tickle my brother, nudging him away from the sleeping Maria.

"The conquistador jumped from the dying horse. He fought the king.

"'What kind of creature is this?' the king wondered as he watched the beast, which had blood spilling from its heaving side. It fell to the ground. The king watched part of it die. But before the king understood what was happening, the top part pulled away from the dead part and moved towards him. The conquistador's sword found the king's heart."

Manuelito's joking stops at this part of the story.

"The king's mistake cost him his life. From that time on, the *quetzal*'s chest has been stained red with the blood of the Mayan king."

Manuelito climbs into Papa's lap.

"We have something to learn from the *quetzal*. We must remember not to make a mistake as the king did," Papa says. My fingers caress the *quetzal* on my blouse that Mama stitched.

"We must be careful who we trust," Manuelito says.

"Yes, son, and we must watch carefully, so that we can't be fooled." Papa puts Manuelito back on to the ground. Trusting his words, Manuelito and I fall asleep with our feet pointed in the direction we will travel in tomorrow.

I dream of a quetzal, which flies away from the bloodstained poacher in the shadows. Abuela has sprouted long, black wings. She flies up from the dirt, straight up into the white sky.

Our Lady reaches out to greet her, but Abuela tumbles to earth, unable to fly high enough.

Before we move off again, Manuelito helps me sweep my pictures clean with branches and leaves. We hide the broken branches in the brush.

For several days, the army seems to be everywhere. It is too dangerous for Papa to look for fruit or roots to eat. Even with the grasses that we munch on, I am hungry. I know Maria and Manuelito are hungry too and I worry about them complaining. Even the smallest noise made with a stick in the dirt could alert a civilian patrol.

Without my loom, or even the earth, I can only draw in my mind. I imagine drawing Catarina running to greet me, Hector raising his fist after scoring a goal, Carlos emerging from the field, Abuela handing me a cup of warm tea, Mama at her loom. The thought of a stick scratching these images in the earth helps me stop trembling.

When we get to the city, things will be different. I know they will be better.

Please, Our Lady, make it so.

✿ ✿ ✿

In my dream, Mama whispers, "Tomasa." Her voice makes the parts of me that were torn and ragged, like a ripped fingernail, feel smooth like a rock in the creek bed, safe with her touch. So safe.

Inside the dream house, I reach up on to the shelf for my doll with the mango orange dress and long, night-black hair. The doll whispers "Body of Christ" for the first time, kneeling with me before the Padre, with the host in my mouth. After a year of preparation for my first holy communion, I walk up the aisle of the church. My doll and I are wearing the same clothes.

And in my dream I am older and it is time for my fifteenth birthday. Mama weaves my doll a new skirt so that she will look like me.

"Mama!" I scream, when she disappears. I run outside, but the path is empty. She has gone.

When I go back into the house I see Abuela waking up. She reaches out. "Pleased to see you again," she says, as she shakes my doll's hand.

Someone shakes my arm. The dream fades to fog. But someone goes on shaking my arm. The hand tightens. My heart races.

Papa. My heart slows as he nudges me until he is sure I am awake. As I sit up, Abuela and my doll dissolve like *dulce de coco* left out in the rain.

It is still night. Papa does not have to say, "We are going." Something has told him we should move on in the dark. I see he has Manuelito. I pick up Maria and follow without a word.

CHAPTER 11

As the sun rises, we look for a good place to rest. Papa lets Manuelito lead us to a place sheltered by brush. I put Maria down. She is as glad to be off my back and walking as I am to be free from her weight for a while.

Maria's movements on her feet have become so steady! She is more and more sure of herself. She will be a big surprise for Mama.

As we camp that night, I watch my father while he is busy with Manuelito. Off our land, away from his field, Papa has changed. His straw hat with its brim turned up on the sides is the same, but the face it shades is not.

Maria lies down and starts to grizzle. I can feel Papa looking at me while I feel her chest under her *huipil*. She is hot.

"I have something special for you," I whisper, as I untie Abuela's bundle and find the herb that stops fever. She bends back her head and seeks out

Papa, then looks at Manuelito while I pinch some of the herb out of the pouch and put it on my tongue. I roll it until it is wet, then push it together into a small worm between my teeth. I hold it up to Maria's mouth. "*Dulce*. Just like sweets," I whisper.

She shakes her head. "No," she tells me. She knows I am lying.

"Señorita Hummingbird, if you eat this, I will ask Papa to tell you about the road covered with beautiful flowers and bright sawdust where the saints are carried." Manuelito moves closer, as I whisper. "Oh, the smell, like heaven with their perfumes." I touch her nose. "And you will not hear a sound when those feet touch the ground. The sawdust and flowers will be jealous and will steal the sound of those marching feet. The flowers will want all the attention."

Manuelito smiles. "And if Manuelito wants to" – I whisper this to Maria and then turn to Manuelito – "we will pick up flowers after the procession." His smile widens.

Even though Maria does not believe that this little herb worm will taste like candy, she opens her mouth and chews. She swallows, and it is not long before she is still. She stares at me as if my face might become Mama's.

Maybe it already has.

Maestro told Papa about a village. He said we will reach it before we get to the town below. He said there are people living there whom we can trust. Papa leaves us on the outskirts. When he finds out if it is true, he will come back for us. We do not know what we would do if it is not true. We do not know what will happen if Papa does not come back. No. That cannot happen.

When Manuelito is sure Papa can no longer hear him he tells me, "I want *tortillas*." Manuelito is not satisfied with what we find to eat in the forest.

"Soon," I say. We finished the last of the *tortillas* the day before yesterday. They were hard and dry. Manuelito complained about them. But now I think even those would be a feast.

He throws a stone.

"No," I tell him.

"You are not Papa," he says.

"And I am not Mama either," I say. "I am your sister. Before you throw another stone, think. What would happen if Papa comes back and we're gone – and all because someone discovered us because you were throwing stones?"

I think he might throw the stone he has in his hand at me.

"I don't care if I never see her again," Manuelito

says, sounding as though he means it.

It makes me sad from my hair to my toes

"She couldn't take us with her," I tell him. "She wanted to, but she couldn't."

He stands poised to throw that stone for another moment. He squeezes it, then releases his hand. The stone falls to the ground with a thud. He comes close and lies down facing away from me, but close enough that I can touch his back while he cries.

I pick up a stick and draw in the dirt. Manuelito turns. He and Maria silently stare at the drawing.

"Spider," Maria whispers.

"Good!" I tell her softly.

I wipe it clean and do the next drawing.

✿ ✿ ✿

When Papa returns, his lips soften from a tight line almost into a smile when he sees we are waiting, safe and quiet.

"The people we need to see are no longer here," Papa says. Manuelito's eyes get bigger. "But I have a *tortilla* for you to share, and tomorrow…" Papa does not finish his sentence.

I tear the *tortilla* into four parts. Papa tears his part into three and gives us each another piece. I tear what he gives me into three and give my pieces to Maria, Manuelito, and Papa. I am glad he accepts this little bit.

I wonder if Mama and Carlos came to this village? I wonder if the kind people were here for them?

Tonight, after the story, after I pray, I have a hard time sleeping. Worry grips me, worry that someone saw Papa looking for friends who would help us.

When day breaks, Maria's fever continues. Abuela's herbs do not cool her shivering body for long. Papa says we must head towards another village to find a healer.

We take apart the branches of the shelter Papa built against the rain and scatter them about. We travel around the other side of the peak.

Towards night, my legs feel so tired, I am sure we have walked around this mountain five times.

✿ ✿ ✿

When we come to the place on the path that leads down, we see the smoke. Too much smoke. More than cooking fires.

I think of our house. This smoke is more than one house, more than one big house.

We head back up to the ridge. Papa keeps us moving away from the smoke.

Finally, we rest by a spring. I kneel down at

the edge of the water. I dip the bottom of my shawl into the small pool, leaving it a minute to soak up water. Then I hold it over Maria's lips. She does not open her mouth. With one finger, I pull her mouth open. With my other hand, I squeeze the cloth slowly so that a few drops trickle into the side of her mouth. After I have done this four times, Papa bends down and touches her forehead with the palm of his hand.

We move on again. Papa walks quickly, and soon Manuelito asks for a ride. Papa bends to scoop him up. He moves on just as quickly. Before the sun is high above us, we turn on to a faint path that brings us down away from the smoke.

" I know of another village beyond this one." Papa means, beyond the one that burns. We can still smell the brown, burnt air.

We walk for several hours before we see a break in the trees. Papa stops. Through the trees lies a great long mound of freshly-turned-over earth. A large yellow machine like the one that they brought to our village stands off to the side, silent.

We stay amongst the trees as we continue along the outskirts of this village. The burnt smell is not fresh, but days old. Some of the buildings have no roofs. We come to a field that has been trampled. We hear the voices and laughter of men. No children's voices. No women's voices. No song.

We see a cooking fire and smell corn and lamb. My stomach growls.

Maria stirs. What if she were to cry out? Papa nods at me, as though he shares my worry. We turn off into the forest, away from the food, away from the hope of medicine or a healer. *What would Mama do? What herbs would Abuela use? Please Our Lady, take away this fever,* I pray, as I move towards the worry that we might have to dig the earth and leave Maria's body behind.

When we stop, far beyond the village, Maria shakes as though she is cold, but her body is still so hot. I rock her until she is still. I doze.

In my dreams I move in darkness. My heart pounds. I wake knowing something is wrong.

Manuelito has vanished. I look carefully in each direction. He has disappeared. I shake Papa. He sits with a start. He looks and listens. I smell our fear.

If a soldier or the civil patrol took Manuelito, they would have taken us all. He must have gone on his own. But where?

Papa gets on to his knees. Slowly he rises to his feet. He moves slowly and quietly, looking hard at the ground, for a clue.

Before Papa moves out of my sight, Manuelito reappears. His hand outstretched, he shows us a plant with a small white flower. "It's best in a tea,"

Manuelito says, as he hands it to me.

I look at Papa, who nods. We risk lighting a small fire.

We have only a metal cup in which to warm the water. I soak the flower and leaves just as Manuelito tells me to. When the water turns a light brown, I add some cool water. I dribble a few drops at a time into Maria's mouth and rub her throat gently, telling her to swallow. She does. Slowly the cup of tea disappears. When the cup is empty, she sleeps still and deep.

Later, when we wake, Maria's fever has gone.

I will never call my brother small again. Manuel has returned Maria to us. Manuel has shed his 'ito'.

CHAPTER 12

Maria stays awake for longer snatches of time. She smiles at Manuel's silly faces. But when she reaches for some of the mushrooms Papa found and starts to eat them, I realise I have not taken a full, deep breath in many days. I do so now, thanking God, Our Lady, and Abuela.

Soon we leave our mountain. Her trees and boulders, ledges and outcrops have protected us in an embrace. I have never been so far down her skirt as we are today. My legs shake after hours of downward trekking.

Papa says, "Let's stop here. It looks like a good place." *Safe place,* is what he means. Since moving from under the cover of the trees, I feel exposed, uncomfortable. But I say nothing.

As we set up a shelter, I wonder: how can you run from a place you love? My mind jumps from one piece of our lives to another, as we cover the spot between two boulders with brush. I think of the colours of the market. I feel the bundle of herbs I handed to the vendor. Smell the pine soap, before I picked up the ash bar and returned to Mama on the blanket. Remember the *thwap* of a foot kicking the soccer ball; the sun shining on me as I washed clothes in the stream; the laughter of the women under the trees' canopy as they work; the smile on Manuel's face as he returned with a bright flower and a pale root from the forest for Abuela; Mama looking into Maria's face; Papa looking into Mama's face; Abuela smiling at me.

Tonight I look straight up into the bright points in the dark sky, holes Our Lady pierced with her needle to let the light shine through the fabric of the sky.

My eyes settle on that small, familiar piece of the sky revealing itself through the canopy of our forest, I see how many more stars shine, neighbours of my home stars.

Papa begins his story as soon as we settle on the ground. We must be ready to rise in a moment. Knowing this is like a thin blanket of thistle that makes me uneasy.

I hear the words, "Once the *quetzal* was green," and I know that Manuel will hear his favourite story. I fall asleep with a smile.

In my dream, the quetzal is green. The King's blood has not yet stained its chest.

CHAPTER 13

Our steps bring us down farther. Cars and trucks move in the distance. When we hear an occasional helicopter or plane, we find cover. It is afternoon when Papa stops behind a rise offering some protection.

"Let me see what is up ahead on that road."

Manuel, Maria and I all lie down. I doze, and before my dreams come, Papa returns.

"Help me gather firewood," he says. "I will trade it for food in the town up ahead." Even Maria, with her wobbly legs, helps. She squats, and with tiny fingers she gathers small sticks for kindling a fire.

When we have a full load, Papa lifts the bundle on to his back. He slips the strap around his forehead and leans forward, his back as flat as a *mesa*. He looks down, planting his feet carefully as he walks away from us.

We stay wide awake, imagining the food he will bring back to us.

"*Tamales*," Manuel says.

"Small *tamales* with black beans," I say.

"Tilla," Maria says. We laugh at her attempt at saying '*tortilla*,' and at her knowing what our stomachs hope is true.

Papa returns without his bundle of wood. I can tell he has good news by the way he tries to hold down his smile.

"Have you found Mama and Carlos?" I ask.

"No, Tomasa. I have not yet asked about them. But there is still time."

"Have you brought us something to eat?" Manuel reaches into Papa's pockets.

"Food is waiting for us, son. Tonight we will sleep with a roof over our heads. We are going to stay with good people. You can call them Tía and Tío."

Mama always told us to tell the truth, "But today," Papa says, "we cannot."

We follow Papa to the town, where he walks as though he grew up in one of the many houses we pass. I have never seen so many houses together, never imagined so many with tin roofs. My feet and legs feel the hardness of the road pounded by so many people and cars and trucks. The smells of cooking and vehicles mix together and I have to breathe it all in.

Soldiers drive towards us in a truck. Papa walks on at a steady pace.

I pray the soldiers cannot hear my heart beating

loud enough to turn the moon white. I watch the road in front of my feet. The soldiers pass, not seeming to notice us even though we look different from the people here who wear shoes and clothes made from store-bought material, thin and light.

Other people wear *huipile*s and woven skirts. Some men wear trousers with patterns from different villages in the highlands, but not many.

I feel loud, as if I am taking up too much space.

Brakes screech behind us. A motor shuts off. Someone shouts *"Alto!"* Papa does not walk faster, even though I want him to run. He does not turn. It is clear from his example that I should not look round, but I do. An army truck has braked at an angle on the road. A soldier questions a man.

Manuel turns. Papa says, "Careful, monkey. Look where you are going, so you do not trip and fall."

We pass two more houses, before Papa turns down a smaller street. The moment before my line of vision is blocked by another house, I see the man who has been questioned. His face wears blood. He is thrown into the back of the truck.

I want to be back in the highlands, where there are plants and trees to cover us. I want to find Mama and Carlos and take them back to our village, the way it was before the soldiers came. I want each house we pass to open its door and pull us in out of this street where I feel watched and out of place.

Finally, Papa stops in front of a house with a blue door painted with flowers. He knocks softly and the door bursts open.

"Hermano!" a woman cries out in a happy voice as if she was greeting her own brother. She ushers us in. Manuel and I look down at the floor, sure that Papa and this crazy woman have made a mistake.

Tía cannot be mistaken for a member of our family. She is *ladina* – so light, next to our brown Mayan skin.

The house has two rooms and a table with chairs. The floor is wooden.

"Come and eat," Tía says. The kindness in her voice makes me less wary. When food is mentioned, Manuel stops staring at the floor. It is hard for me not to snatch at the *tortilla* wrapped around warm beans, hard to resist grabbing like a starving animal that has been kept so long from cooked food. My mouth greets each bite that gradually satisfies my growling stomach. Before we have finished, a dark-skinned man walks through the door.

"Look, husband, our brother has come with his *familia*."

"It is good to see you again," this man we are supposed to call Tío says to us all. He looks like us. "Let me eat, and then you can come work with me in my field." He now speaks only to Papa, "While we work, you can tell me about your journey."

Once we are all full up, the men leave the house.

Tía says, "I could use some help fetching water from the well. It is not far. Just down the road a bit." I stand up to go with her. "No, I think I need a strong boy for this task." She moves her hands in a way that tells me to sit back down. Manuel jumps up.

"Do you mind if I take Maria as well?" Tía says. Papa told us to trust this woman, but I am not sure. When I hesitate, she says, "But no, she looks like she's ready for a nap. Maybe it would be better if you have a nap with her while Manuel and I go. Would that be OK?"

I nod.

I lie down on a blanket with Maria in the corner, where two walls shelter me like a cave. I sleep, with no dreams.

I wake to movement and I sit up, remembering I am in the house in town. Maria splashes in a metal tub. Manuel helps Tía move a pot from the fire. Tía takes a scoop of the hot water and adds it to the metal tub.

She smiles at me. "You look better," she says. "But you will look even better after you've washed."

I look at my feet. Dust covers my ankles in thick socks. Tía sends Manuel out to the back to break the smaller branches into even smaller pieces.

I slip into the tub. The water and soap cleans away more than the dust. I feel lighter as I move the soap over my shoulders. I imagine my worries sliding off my skin and dissolving in the now-grey water.

✿ ✿ ✿

Soon after Tía and I start to prepare the evening meal, Papa and Tío come back. My stomach is purring. It cannot believe its luck to get another meal so soon.

Papa sits down at the table. He does not say it, but just as simple things like taking a bath and preparing a meal with Tía have been special for me, his work in the field today has been special for him.

"Tomorrow, Manuel can come with us." Papa says.

"Today your Papa helped me get the field ready," Tío says. "All the leaves we took from the corn will keep our cow happy. Tomorrow we will plant Chinese peas for market. Corn again in May, just as there was in your papa's field."

Later, in the darkness, I listen to the quiet voices of the grown-ups.

"You do not want to go to Guatemala City," Tía says. "The only job you will find is carrying 125-pound bags of sugar or coffee. It won't be worth the *quetzals* you earn or the danger you might face; soldiers are there looking for people fleeing the highlands."

Tío says. "There are places in Mexico City where you find kind hearts who will help."

"I thought we would stay in Guatemala City or Antigua until my wife and son return," Papa says. "They may be in Guatemala City now."

Papa says something too low for me to hear. Tía answers in a soft stream of words I cannot understand. I sit up and move closer so that all of their words find me.

Tío and Tía see me, pause, and look at Papa. He nods his approval for me to hear what they will say next.

"It is different from the trouble you know in the highlands, but it is much the same," Tío says.

"Last week a boy spray-painted *Libertad* on a wall in the capital, and they shot him," Tía says. "He died on the pavement alone, just for writing the word *freedom*."

I picture the street where this happened.

"I understand he was trying to shout the word out loud," says Tío, "so that maybe others would hear, be brave and help. But it was a foolish thing to do. We need to stay alive, to work for our freedom."

There are more words about road-blocks and

kidnappings, instructions on how to travel on buses, and a warning never to speak about what happened in our village or the freshly-covered mound we saw in the village with all the soldiers. Finally, they stop talking, and sleep calls me.

I dream about a boy spray-painting a word on the wedding-cake palace wall. Dressed in white, he walks along the pavement carpeted with flowers like the photographs the teacher showed us. I walk along the hard street towards him.

I want to know how he makes this magic from a tin of paint. I want to be brave enough to stand beside him. I do not understand what it is he wants, but I know what I want. I want to be back at home, the way things used to be before the soldiers came.

The boy in my dream looks like Hector. He tells me gently not to step on the flowers, so I stay in the street watching.

Before the last black letter is finished, a crack slaps the air from behind the crowd. The boy with the tin of paint turns to see what has happened. He hits the wall where the letters are still wet, and the word "freedom" smears as he slides down silently on the flowery pavement. He lies in a puddle of black that has stained the white flowers.

I turn and see Manuel reaching down and picking up one of the dripping flowers.

"No!" I scream.

The crowd says nothing, because none of them have any lips. People scatter to avoid the next bullet.

CHAPTER 14

Papa and Manuel leave after breakfast to work in the field with Tío. I feel as though a piece of me goes with them. I worry about what Manuel might say or do. I worry from a distance. Mama must be doing the same thing. But she has been doing it twice as long as we have.

As we finish preparing the *masa*, there is a knock. The door opens. I swoop Maria up into my arms.

"Oh, look, Tomasa and Maria," Tía says in a light voice, "your cousins have arrived! You probably cannot remember them. You were so young when you saw them last." Tía faces me. *You are safe*, she says with her smile. Then she turns to the two women who have just come in.

Maria squirms in my arms. When I put her back down on the floor, she stands behind me, holding my legs.

To the women, Tía says, "Daughters, look who has come to visit. Look how my *sobrina* Tomasa has grown since we last saw her."

The woman at the door has a new baby on her back. She looks Mayan like her father. The pregnant one has a boy who looks Maria's age. Their skin is lighter, like Tía's. Both women carry red buckets.

The pregnant one who came in first smiles and embraces me, and then stands back. "Tomasa, you've grown so much, I almost didn't recognise you!" She touches me on the shoulders, smiles and looks me over.

Worry clouds the black eyes of the other sister standing at the door. Her mouth holds no welcome. She stands in front of the painted flowers on the door, shielding me from outside eyes as she closes the door. Once the door is securely shut, she turns. "This isn't something to joke about," she says in a hissing whisper.

Tía picks up two deep-red pails of her own. "Oh, daughter, I know this is not a game. We do what we must for these children. They aren't to blame for what's happening. I'm only doing what I hope someone would do for our family, if we had walked such a long way. Come now. Time to go for water. We don't want to miss out on the gossip at the well."

I reach out to help with one of the pails.

"She should stay here," the daughter at the door says. "You should think about your own family."

Everyone stops talking and stares at me. The pregnant woman with the boy breaks the silence.

"Tomasa, my *hijo* Juan would be good company for this little one," she says, squatting down to touch Maria's head. "Would you mind looking after them both while we get water? It would give me a rest." I nod my agreement, glad I will not be with them.

Tía comes to take the container from me. As she hugs me, she whispers, "Don't let the things she says worry you."

But they do.

✧ ✧ ✧

Later that morning, after her daughters have left, Tía asks, "Did you make this beautiful skirt?"

"Mama did," I say. She must know that a girl my age could not make a fabric so fine. Tía reaches out and feels the patches.

Hidden under one patch is our money. Under one of the others are our identification cards, giving the name of our village. If this name reached the wrong ears, they would know that our village has been burnt down. A soldier at a checkpoint would know that most of the people did not leave it. He would have been told about the machine they sent to cut into the earth, making the ground ready for our stubbornness.

In a soldier's hands, our identification cards would say that we came from a place where the people did not hide from the dark noisy helicopter that *thwap, thwap thwaped* around and around our village, that we came from a place where *la gente* did not flee from the guns. After seeing our identification cards, a soldier would be certain that any story we told him would be a lie.

So we have to avoid soldiers.

"Your mama is a fine weaver," is all Tía says, but I know that her fingers have found the hidden identification cards.

Before she can speak, I blurt out, "Do you know if my mother and brother have travelled this way?"

"I wish I could give you some news of them, but I have none," Tía says. She talks to me as she would talk to her daughters, as though I am old enough to understand. "When you get closer to the border, it will be safer for you to leave these clothes behind and wear more ordinary clothes bought from a shop."

Leave these clothes that Mama's hands created? Abandon the design her heart told her fingers to paint on the threads of her loom? Wearing Mama's work makes me feel her close to me. But I must resist such childish thoughts. I must give up the clothes.

"If I had a beautiful cloth like this made by my mother, I would keep it wrapped up in my bundle," Tía says. "I think you must keep this one. But why not let me buy Maria's skirt and the beautiful *huipil*es you wear for my grandchildren?"

"Please let me give them to you." I know Mama would approve of this, in return for Tía's kindnesses of shelter and food.

"Such fine embroidery," Tía says. "Let me give you something in return." She walks to the far wall and pulls open a drawer in a wooden cabinet. "What have we here that would fit you?"

The drawer is filled with skirts and blouses, plain ones. The fabric between my fingers feels delicate, as though it would not survive nights on the ground. Again Tía answers my thoughts.

"These clothes might not last as well as what you are wearing. You'd better take two. They are light. You will not even notice the extra weight." She pulls a few out and holds them up against me. "Maybe it would be better if they were a little bigger so you have room to grow."

I blush.

When Maria and I have two sets of clothes, Tía opens a second drawer with trousers and shirts for boys.

We pull some out that we think would fit Manuel and Papa.

"Now let me see how big your feet are," Tía says. "Paved roads will seem softer if you're wearing shoes."

She puts brown paper down on the floor and asks me to stand on it. With a pencil she traces my foot, going back and forth. It tickles. I laugh.

My heart feels lighter when Papa and Manuel return. Tía asks Manuel to stand on the paper next to where my foot is drawn. She does not tickle him. When Tío leaves with one of the bundles of firewood they brought back with them, he also takes the paper.

Tía and I begin to cook. Before we are done, Tío returns. He gives Papa *quetzals* for the firewood.

"This is too much," Papa says, handing some of the money back.

Tío refuses.

Papa puts his head down, folds it and puts it in his pocket. "*Gracias.*"

Tío takes off the string pack he wears over his shoulder. He pulls shoes out of the bag and hands Manuel and me each a pair. The leather on the pair he hands me is thinner and shows more wear than the leather of Manuel's.

"Maybe you could put them on, so your feet can get used to them," Tía says.

I put on each shoe and stand up. My feet feel as if they are carrying houses, the way a turtle carries a shell.

"I had to leave my boots behind to be mended," barefooted Tío says to Papa. He bends down and pulls worn shoes from under the cabinet and hands them to Papa. "I hope you will take these old ones off my hands."

"It is enough that the children have them," Papa says.

"Trust me. I cannot let my brother travel to Mexico without these lucky shoes."

Manuel is surprised to hear about Mexico. He whispers, "What about the procession with flowers in Guatemala City?"

"Maybe they celebrate with flowers in Mexico." I do not know what else to say.

✧ ✧ ✧

After dinner Tía says, "Thank you for coming to visit us," as she pours both men an amber drink. "I hope you will remember us to your wife and son when you find them."

I fall asleep to the sound of Tío teaching Papa words that he already knows in a different way.

"...more breath at the end of the word," Tío says.

In my dream, the daughter with the baby on her back is banging on the door marked with flowers. Mama and Tía do not seem to notice the knocking as they sit together sewing patches as delicate as a spider's web all over the store-bought clothes.

The patches they sew come from Mama's loom.

"Looooom," Tía says.

"Loooooooom." I repeat.

✿ ✿ ✿

As the sun wakes, Tía and Tío hug each of us before we go through the blue-flowered door. We leave long before their daughters arrive.

"Que te vaya bien," Tía says. "May it go well for you."

"K'awilawib, take care," Tío says, the way Mama and Abuela would have said goodbye.

Papa seems to know exactly where he is going. The paved road feels hard under the soles of my shoes. I am glad I do not have to worry about the broken glass that lies along the roadside. With each step, I think only of avoiding soldiers.

We reach the outskirts of the town quickly and find the road that leads us north to Mexico. Maria relaxes into sleep on my back. Before long, Papa leads us from this road to a path beside it. It takes us to another path that follows the direction of the road.

Did Mama and Carlos walk along this path? I feel them so strongly here that I think they might have. We must be getting closer. I walk with a new sureness, an echo of Papa's.

Even though Tía said we still face danger, I feel as though we are safer dressed in *ladino* clothes with shoes on our feet. But it is not too many hours before Manuel asks to take his shoes off. My feet know why. Papa agrees we should all give our feet a chance to feel the earth again. I wiggle my toes, tie the shoes together and hang them over the backpack Manuel wears. When Papa takes a turn carrying Maria, I take the backpack from Manuel. I am as light as a feather without Maria. The skirt Mama wove presses against my back in the backpack. I feel her courage.

✧✧✧

This morning, as I gather my hair and braid the strands, I wonder if it is true that my hair will fall out now that we have left the highlands. I measure the thickness of my finished braid with my fingers. My thumb and first finger do not quite meet where the braid is thickest at my neck. I think of strands falling on to the road as we walk.

As the sun goes down, the moon peeps over the mountains we once lived on. They seem so far away, so tiny. I know how many steps separate us from them.

"Before I start the story," Papa says, "put your shoes back on."

He means we may have to get up and move on

in the middle of the night. Inside my chest, the thin feeling of safety I wove at Tío and Tía's home starts to rip.

The moon wears her shawl over the right side of her face, covering her eye. Each night for the next few days she will grow shyer. We must wait for her to feel brave again, on the other side of her shyness.

Out of the mountains, I too feel shyer. Here, where it is dangerous to whisper even the name of our village, a smile or sudden tears make me stand out. Away from our home, I must keep my deepest self hidden. This seems impossible. I am always waiting for something to happen.

But my attention turns to the moon. Tonight she does not look well. She is yellow, not white, as she pulls free from the earth. If we were in our village, we would go out and shout. We would bang our pots and make as much noise as we could to make her well again. I watch the moon as she rises higher. What will happen to the moon if no one saves her?

As she rises higher, the sick colour fades. I can almost hear the clatter of noise *la gente* must be making somewhere to help her shine white again, bathing the dark sky with her soft light.

In my mind, I draw the sharp lines of things I hope will not change: my braid thick on my back, the love of my family.

In my dream, I reach out to hold my waiting Mama. But she vanishes, and I end up struggling with shouts and cries and cracks, the sound of machines digging the earth, and flashes of white in the darkness.

✿ ✿ ✿

On the first part of our journey, when we were in the highlands, Manuel, Maria and I saw only each other and Papa. Now we see other people all the time.

We saw buses in the town of the blue door, but Manuel, Maria and I have never ridden in one. Papa explains, "On a bus we will reach *la frontera* more quickly,"

We trudge back up an embankment to the road and walk along it. Papa speaks to a man who is not dressed for work in the fields.

"I am going to the bus now," the man says. "Come with me." We follow him and wait in a place where others are gathered. The fingernails of the woman standing next to me flash red like the chest of a *quetzal*. Maria stiffens when the bus bounces, wheezes and shouts its way towards us. The bus squeals to a stop near where we stand and the door slaps open with a *clush* sound. Maria hides her head and cries.

"We are going to ride, to rest our feet," I tell her. She squeezes me as if her hand could stop me from taking her up the steps.

"She thinks this bus is a monster," Manuel says.

"Ah, but wait until she sees how fast we go," Papa says. "Then I don't think she will mind too much. Her legs will get some rest." Then even Manuel laughs because we know Maria hardly walks at all when we are travelling.

But the bus does look like a green, yellow and orange monster.

When all the people have climbed into the bus, we follow. Papa pays the driver and the door closes. The seats are full and people stand in the aisle. The engine roars and grinds. We jerk back and forth. I lose my balance and fall against a woman sitting with two chickens in a cage on her lap. The birds squawk and flap their wings uselessly. Small feathers fly. One rests on my lips. One escapes up my nose.

The boy in front of me pulls me back up. I do not have time to tell him *"Gracias"* before the chicken woman nods her head to the back of her seat. "Hold on there."

"Move back!" the driver shouts.

I hold on to the seat of the old woman and take a step towards the back where the boy stands. Row by row, I reach for the back of the next seat. When I can go no farther, I stop. A white man and a woman with yellow hair sit in the seat next to where I stand.

Even sitting, they are taller than I am standing. These are probably the first white people Manuel has ever seen. He was young when the missionaries visited our village.

Maria does not seem to notice. Her sobbing has slowed down. She turns and stops crying. Her face looks surprised and unhappy.

"*Está bien.*" I say, as if my telling her that it is good will make it so.

But it is not good. Maria retches. She throws up on me and on the floor. The people around me do not seem to notice. The smell makes my stomach churn. I hear retching behind me and feel the splatter of Manuel's vomit on my ankle.

I think I would rather have walked.

I swallow hard and risk looking out the window. We pass another bus on the side of the road. What I see makes my stomach feel even worse.

The empty bus faces towards the border. People stand on the side of the road. Soldiers cluster at the head of the line like flies around a latrine.

I look back at Papa and Manuel who are staring straight ahead as if they did not see the stopped bus, as ours continues to bump along towards Mama and Carlos, carrying us towards a safer place.

When we finally get off the bus, Maria grizzles, then falls asleep. Papa is carrying Manuel. As sleep pulls Manuel farther away, he jerks awake, half-opens his eyes and then closes them again, his head wobbling on Papa's shoulder.

My legs tremble as they reach for the ground, which seems to be rocking. I am glad my feet did not have to walk the distance we travelled today, but I am happy to be off the bus.

Papa finds us a place to camp close to a stream, so that we can clean ourselves up.

I dream of vomit, empty buses and of the boy on the bus who helped steady me when I lost my balance.

CHAPTER 15

In the morning, we start walking again, beginning the pattern of our day as Mama might begin a new line on the loom. Each footstep is like a string wrapped by a thread, marking another piece of our journey. Only God knows how large the fabric will grow or how long our lives will be. If my prayers are heard, we will be with Mama and Carlos before it is finished. I wish I knew what kind of images we will weave between now and then.

Sometimes, after a night when we hear shooting, we hide all day. The following day we walk away from the road. At other times, we walk along the road as if we are on our way to market.

Oh, and the market we saw yesterday! Three colours of *tortillas*, black beans, fava beans, *chayote*. There were chickens and *chilecayotes*, toasted and ground squash seeds, chicken *tamales*, plenty of greens and wild mustard. Peppers, cabbage, celery, tomatoes, bananas, mangoes and pineapples. I could not pull my eyes away from their reds and greens and yellows.

Today, we are gathering wood. When Papa returns to our camp, before the sun has moved on in the sky, he carries three eggs. A feast!

✿ ✿ ✿

We have not eaten for a day when we reach the place where Guatemala and Mexico touch. At this spot, a river flows between these friends. I know Guatemala touches the ocean: I have seen photographs in Maestro's book. I know the blue thread reaches to the three pyramids across an even bigger water, but I have never seen as much as this. We will need to cross this swollen river on the bridge ahead.

As we reach the Mexican side of the bridge, we wait in a line. People are quiet while they wait. Some stand. Several sit on their haunches. A baby cries. Maria pulls away from my skirt to try to see who is making such a sad, hungry sound. We ache with emptiness in our bellies.

"I am so hungry," Manuel whispers close to my ear.

"Soon," I tell him.

One by one, family by family, the people standing in line talk to the Mexican official who sits behind the tall counter. When it is our turn, Papa tells another lie. "We are going to shop with these *pesos* my sister in Mexico City sent us." Papa holds out the Mexican coins and bills he has been holding since our stay with Tío. He speaks in Spanish using the accent I have heard him practise.

Maria, Manuel and I stand quietly, as we always do in front of strangers. We do not speak, in order to cover up who we are, the way Papa and Manuel covered our belongings at the edge of the jungle before we left.

I know Mama and Carlos wait somewhere on the other side of the line, *la frontera*. We stand in front of the officer from Mexico who sits behind his counter looking down at his papers. He sits between us and *el otro lado*. Papa finishes talking.

The officer looks up. His eyes search each of our faces. "No," he says. He will not let us stay on this side. "Next!" he shouts.

My eyes must show surprise at his "no". I keep my fear of going back across the bridge tucked inside my backpack, under the patch I've sewn on the weak place. I hide my terror of the jagged, threatening letters and of the soldiers who eat at my country as squirming maggots eat the carcass of a dead deer.

We leave the building, past the line of people hoping for a yes.

"Don't worry, *niños*," Papa says, eyes straight

ahead as we cross the bridge. "We will find your Mama and brother."

I think he says it as much for himself as he does for Manuel, Maria, and me.

"I don't care if I never see her again." Manuel whispers to me, so Papa will not hear.

"She could not take us," I tell him.

"She took Carlos," Manuel answers.

The next part comes out louder than I wish. "She wanted to take us all. But she could not." Immediately I am sorry I spoke. The expression on Papa's face does not change. If he did hear me, he would understand what made me say this.

❁ ❁ ❁

On the Guatemalan side of the river, we leave the road where the low bushes meet taller trees. Papa asks me to pull the thread away from one of the patches in my skirt.

I take the skirt from the backpack and unroll it. I pull at a thread, slip the money out and hand it to him.

When Papa comes back, he tells us that we must find coyotes.

"Why would tracking coyotes help us?" Manuel asks. I smile.

"The men who help you cross the river," Papa explains, "they are called coyotes."

I hope they have nothing in common with the coyote from Papa's story who tricked an old starving dog and jaguar out of a piece of bread.

We walk away from the border and soon, we find the men.

"Right this way," a coyote with a red shirt says. He bows as he gestures to the back of the truck. There sits the boy we saw on the bus. The boy nods to us and moves closer to the cab, giving us plenty of room. He probably does not want to risk his shoes in case Manuel and Maria are sick again. The engine roars into life. We bounce along a dirt road with trees on each side.

The truck stops with a jerk. The driver points to a thicket away from the river.

"Get comfortable there. Someone will come for you."

We wait for other coyotes to take us across the river. A truckload at a time, new people arrive. We meet other families, families from El Salvador, Nicaragua and Honduras. So Guatemalans are not the only people who are afraid!

We play together, all children speaking different languages, Quiché, Mam, Tzutujil, Spanish and others that even Papa's ears have never heard before.

We run and chase each other. We smile and play, without needing words. We try to catch each other, until Papa snaps his fingers.

When he snaps, Manuel, Maria and I freeze. The other children freeze as well. A truck approaches, louder than the coyote's. In a second, we all disappear silently into the bush.

We stay hidden until we no longer hear the slow-moving truck on the road. When it feels safe, people reappear. I tear my blouse on a branch as I untangle myself from the bush.

Conversations begin among the adults. Manuel, Maria and another child make designs with small, smooth stones. I move closer. Papa sits next to a man named Felipe, a Mayan who wears city clothes. He rolls a cigarette and offers one to Papa, who says no. When he turns his head, I see that he has a jagged red line where his left ear should be.

My discomfort is interrupted. We all turn towards the anger erupting in a nearby group.

Someone calls out a bad name. The boy from the bus stands up.

"We know who you are," one of the mothers says, pointing a finger at him.

"I did not want to be a soldier," the boy tells the people gathered around him. "They took me from our family's field. They told me they would kill my father, they would rape my sisters and mother, if I did not come with them."

"And whose father and brothers did you kill? Which of our sisters and mothers did you rape?" she says.

"That is why I am here," the boy says. "Do you see me carrying a gun or a machete?"

"Maybe you will wait for us to fall asleep, and then call in your patrol and have us all murdered. Or maybe you will just cut off our ears as a trophy?" she says, pointing in Felipe's direction.

"You're wrong," the boy says. He moves away and sits by himself.

"We are watching you." The woman says again.

✿ ✿ ✿

Now I listen to Felipe. I flatten the dirt with my hands as far as I can reach in front of where I squat.

"Across from the United States Embassy in Guatemala City, there is a place where you stand in line. Men have typewriters on the top of the wall. For five *quetzals* they type the forms for you. I had to pay them to do it for me," Felipe says.

I draw bricks for the wall as he tells stories of how the typewriter men try to help, but cannot do it for free. "They need to click clack on those machines and take money from you, in order to feed their families."

As Felipe tells us about the things you have to tell the typewriter men who prepare your papers for the Embassy, I draw a piece of paper on top of the wall.

He talks about the people who stand in line. "Some of them come from the city. Some work in factories making cars. Some are teachers. One I talked to was a journalist who asked the wrong questions. Some of them have money," Felipe says, "but they are frightened too."

I draw stick people standing one behind another. I put a book in the hand of the third waiting person.

"I stood with a man from the city who feeds his family by standing there all day," he continues. I add another person to the line. I wait for Felipe to say more, so I can understand how a man can feed his family by doing nothing.

"That man is paid to stand in line for someone else. He waits, so that you can work for more money than he charges you. Everywhere you wait, people will offer to stand in line for you."

I draw more stick figures waiting for the typewriter men.

"And then a soldier came with a camera. I saw him take photographs of the Embassy that is bigger on top than it is on the bottom." Felipe has attracted more listeners. Several women have moved closer.

He nods to them, as they sit in our circle. "And then the soldier turned and took photographs of the people standing in line," Felipe says.

A woman from the highlands says, "They did that when I was there."

"They try to scare you," a city woman says, smoothing her thin arched eyebrow with her finger whose nail is painted pink. "If you want to leave, they say you must have done something wrong."

"So they take a photograph and pass it on to the army," Felipe says.

"Or maybe the camera is only taking pretend photos," the city woman says.

"It does not matter." Felipe says, "It makes the line shorter."

The women nod.

Felipe continues, "When the soldier took out the camera, I left, and went back the next day."

I draw the soldier holding a small box in front of his face.

"The second day, it rained in the morning. By midday, I was dry. Soldiers drove by slowly. One shouted 'Communist!' Another snarled 'Guerrilla!' and 'Subversive!' They spat on my face" – Felipe wiped his cheek as if it was still wet – "and the line moved so slowly that I never got inside the building."

I poke dots of rain into my drawing: lots of rain, to wash away what the soldier spat on Felipe. I steal a glance at the boy from the bus. Squatting, his back hunched, he moves his finger in a slow circle in the dirt. He could be lost in his own thoughts, but I wonder if he is listening.

"Night came, and I had to get off the street before the curfew," Felipe says.

"Ah, that happened to me as well," the city woman says. "Thank God I had somewhere to stay. My friends let me stay in their apartment when I discovered someone watching my house." I consider this, until Felipe rescues me from these thoughts.

"So on the third day I waited, the soldiers came to the line and asked people questions. I knew they would not shoot us there in front of the Embassy, but they pulled one woman from the line and dragged her towards their car. She put her legs on the tyre and the back door of the car. It took two of them to shove her in," Felipe's voice trembled.

"I've heard stories of how some people apply and then disappear," the city woman says.

"My husband went in to answer questions," the woman from the highlands says in a small voice. "He never came home."

"I am sorry," Felipe says. He turns back to Papa, "So I left the line. I think it is better to go without papers." Felipe rolls another cigarette. Again he offers it to Papa, who refuses.

"My husband was told to bring in his papers to the police station," another woman says. "They promised they would clear things up so we could apply for a visa."

No one answers. As she weeps, the city woman moves to sit next to her.

"Maybe he has already gone across," the city woman tells her. "Maybe he will meet you."

I scratch back and forth over my drawing. Gone is the wall with the typewriter on top. Starting with the one who stands behind the other, I wipe out each person in my dirt line standing straight and stick thin — the line waiter, the car-maker, the teacher reading a book, Felipe, the woman's husband, Mama and Carlos. I scratch out the soldier taking the photo and all the drops of rain which cleaned the spit from Felipe's cheek. All those brown images mix and zig-zag like dark lightning across the dirt.

I wipe at the tears that escape without my knowing. I look up. The boy from the bus has turned round. He is looking at me.

CHAPTER 16

On the second day in this camp near the river, people are starting to grumble. "We should not have given them any money until we reached Mexico," Felipe says.

The city woman pulls a newspaper out of her bag again. I long to read, to drink in words that have been denied us on our journey. After a while, she notices me watching.

"Here, have the pages I've finished with." I sit next to her and pore over the images. First, a football game, two men in formal city clothes shaking hands. She helps me with the words I do not recognise. The newspaper tells of football games and peace talks. It says the guerrillas have killed a lot of people in the highlands. It says that soldiers have been sent there 'to protect the people'. I think about our goat. I think about our village. I want to ask questions, but I know that would anger Papa. I give the newspaper back.

By the third evening, one coyote dressed in a dirty

white T-shirt and blue jeans comes back and we follow him down a rutted path. From this spot, one group at a time is called. After many hours, all the families except ours and the boy from the bus have left. It is our turn to climb on to the four boards covering a big truck tyre tube that will take us over the fast-moving river. A rope reaches out across the river to two men who stand on the Mexican side.

The river sounds hungry. The boy climbs on. The outside piece of wood covering the tyre is loose. The boy wobbles for a moment. He almost loses his balance, until the board he kneels on relaxes and drops to lie flat against the tyre. The coyote stands on a piece of rope between the coil on the bank and where the rope is tied on to the tyre. He keeps the raft steady while his arms are free to help.

I am frightened when Papa hands the last of our money to the coyote, who motions for Papa to climb on. Papa's foot slips and he stands in the water. Quickly, he pulls himself up on to the wet boards next to the boy. Papa reaches out for Manuel as the coyote helps my brother from the ground.

The coyote turns to me. He lifts Maria from my arms and pushes her towards Papa's outstretched ones. I move towards the raft, but I am stopped short by the coyote's arm shooting out across my chest. I push him away. He picks me up and puts me down, away from the river bank. He calls to another coyote.

"Put my daughter on." Papa's sharp words catch the attention of the boy from the bus, who has been looking across the river. The boy turns. In an instant he sees what is happening. He jumps into the river and moves around the side of the raft. His hands never let go of the boards, so that the raft will not leave without me.

The coyote signals across the river and the men wave back and pull at the rope. The raft jerks away from the shore. Papa reaches towards the rope, jumps back into the river and pulls the raft back towards the shore.

"Hurry up," the coyote yells into the bush to his friend. Together the boy and Papa are able to hold the raft still while the others across the river keep pulling. This leaves the coyote's hands free to pull me away from the shore.

"Tell them to stop pulling," the boy says, as though he were a general.

The coyote ignores him and continues to pull me, even though I dig my shoes into the dirt. The trail of my feet leaves two thin ruts.

"Stop them pulling the rope," the boy demands again.

I bite the coyote.

He screams, and reaches out to hit me with his

free arm. He lets go with the hand I have just cut with my teeth.

Freed, I fly towards the raft, and Papa lifts me on and jumps up to sit next to me. Manuel puts his arm around my shoulder. Maria climbs into my lap.

"There are too many people. The raft is too low in the water," the coyote says defensively.

"Could it be that you wanted to keep this one?" the boy says, motioning to me.

The thought of the coyote keeping me makes my stomach feel sicker than that bus ride.

The coyote's friend bursts out of the brush and on to the bank. "What's going on?"

The boy plants his feet between the raft and the coyotes. "I will wait for the next crossing," the boy says, as though he was a soldier still.

The coyotes obey his order.

✿ ✿ ✿

Just as I settle down, the loose board shifts and my right foot slips between the boards. I try not to look down, but when I do, I see the water just a hand away from me. I tremble, the way I did when I said goodbye to Abuela. We hold on tight. I feel the tug on the rope, the tug that pulls us across the water, water that rushes beneath us. I shut my eyes tight and pray.

The rope jerks. My fingers have cramped. I cannot hold on any tighter. I cannot swim, nor can my brother or sister. I do not know if Papa can. But even if he can, could he save us all if we ended up in the water?

If I were to weave tonight, my pattern would show the line of dark water with cold brown hands reaching up to pull me under.

A violent jerk of the rope sends me too close to the edge. Close to the water. What's happening?

I look back. The boy grabs the rope. The coyote jerks again.

The raft is rocking. Water sloshes on to the edges that dip into the water with each sway.

The coyote must be trying to knock us into the water.

The boy swings out an arm. He connects with the coyote's stomach. When the coyote strikes back, the rope drops and the tyre tube catches the current and spirals down the river instead of across it.

"Hold on tight," Papa says.

I look back towards the shore. The boy and the coyote slip from view. We pick up speed and travel farther and farther towards the middle of the flow. We reach the point where the rope is in a straight line from the Mexico coyotes, and we move more and more towards their shore.

We head for a rock jutting out of the water.

We hit it before I can say, "Be careful."

Manuel looses his balance. He rolls over the side and falls into the water. The backpack rolls off too. Papa reaches for Manuel and grabs him just in time. The backpack bobs away. Maria howls.

"Shssh. We are OK, Hummingbird," I say to calm her. "Papa will bring Manuel back."

Papa pulls Manuel in as the rope jerks against the current. They are both caught off guard. Papa catches his balance while Manuel's knee, which has found its way to the edge of the board, slips and he slides towards the water. Papa steadies himself and hauls Manuel in a second time.

As the raft is slowly pulled towards the coyotes on the Mexican side, Papa keeps pushing us away from the brush and tree branches which have fallen in the water's edge.

We hold on tight. I ignore the splinters.

The raft moves in a steady rhythm. I imagine the men on the Mexican side, pulling arm over arm as the raft jerks through the water.

Then we slow. We stop. My eyes follow the rope from the raft as it points in the direction we want to go. Down in the water something has snagged it. Something underwater holds us back.

Papa reaches for the rope. He pulls from our end. Then side-to-side. Finally he tries up and down.

Papa uses his hand to paddle and push us towards the spot where the rope disappears into the water. His hands are not strong enough to push against the rush of the water.

"Hold on tight," Papa tells us again, and he pushes his legs into the water and kicks the rope to loosen it. Even that does not free us.

Papa jumps into the water, holding on to the side. He pulls the rope.

"NO!" Manuel shouts, as Papa takes a deep breath and disappears under water. He comes up spluttering. Then, gulping in fresh air, he disappears again.

He breaks out of the water, and takes another deep breath. Up and down, twice more. Each rest is longer.

Finally we are free. The raft begins to move. Papa follows along holding on to the rope. His legs move out behind him – I can see them floating under the surface of the water. Manuel reaches out to steady Papa. I move to the other side to balance our weight. Papa grips the side of the boards and carefully lifts himself back on, without knocking us off. He pulls hard on the rope to let the people on the Mexican side know we are free. But now we are moving in the wrong direction. Papa pulls on the rope – and at last the raft moves down the middle of the river. We pick up speed.

The raft bobs and spins.

Maria howls again.

We bounce off two more rocks before Papa moves us on to three of the boards which are tied together. He pushes the end of the loose fourth board into the water. He holds it flat against the pull. We slow down. Papa uses the board to move the raft away from Guatemala's shore toward Mexico. But he is not that strong and the bend in the river pulls us towards the wrong side.

Papa rows and rows until he cannot row any more. He loses the oar and it floats away. The raft comes close to a tree and we grab on to its branches.

Papa pulls us to shore and we climb off. I look across to where I wish we were, but I am grateful to feel earth under our feet.

The board Papa used in the water is lost. He unties the three boards and carries them. He wears the loop of rope around his shoulder. Manuel helps to roll the tube. I follow with Maria in my arms. After an hour of walking, we return to the coyote's camp.

I am relieved to see there are other families waiting.

"You stole our raft!" the coyote says. I look around for the boy. He is nowhere to be seen.

"I did not steal it," Papa answers.

"You owe me for the money we lost while you took our raft," the coyote says.

"You let go," Papa said. "The coyote already has the money for our trip."

"You must help us make boards to replace what you lost, and you must help us with the pulling, to repay me for all the money I could have made while you were sightseeing."

I do not want to be left at the camp with the coyotes, so even though the ride on the river and the walk back have taken all my strength, Manuel, Maria and I follow Papa. He finds a tree that will give us the board we need. He prays, asking the tree for forgiveness for taking its life. He promises the tree it will be used well. And then he chops it down with his machete.

✿ ✿ ✿

Papa works all night and into the next day pulling the rope, loading people, pulling the rope again. Even though he has been using his shirt to protect his hands, the palms bleed before he has earned our passage.

Even though I am tired, I fight sleep as we wait for our turn. Maria grizzles. Everyone in the coyote's camp freezes when they hear the sound of a motorboat. Papa helps the coyote pull things away from the shore's edge. They use branches to cover up the footprints in the mud.

Maria cries.

"Shut her up," a man says.

I rock her and whisper in her ear, "Hummingbird, soon we will be in Mexico. Soon we will see Mama. Carlos will tickle your toes."

"Stop moving. You'll give us all away," the man hisses.

A woman with grey hair moves up to be next to me. She shows me a brown liquid. "This will make her sleep," the woman says.

The woman pours a few drops on to Maria's tongue. She stops crying and looks at my face. It must taste good!

"A little more," the woman says.

Maria drinks greedily.

She falls asleep even before the boat reaches us with its motor *putt-putting*, bright light searching the shoreline first on one side and then the other. The light does not reach far back into the brush where we hide. The crossings are called off for several hours. Manuel joins Maria for a nap. I cannot fight sleep any longer.

In my dream, I float past ordinary scenes in black and white, in the market, at my loom, tickling Maria with the tail feather of a quetzal. Along the river of images I snag on the white flames licking at our house. There we are, squatting in the field, moving quickly into the mountain's wild places, coming down again. The only way out is over the fresh mound outside the burned village that gives way under my foot. The mound eats my leg up to the knee. As the firm hold of those fingers pulls me down, I feel the hand of the greedy coyote clutching at my arm. Now we are on the river. Hands in the water try to knock us from our raft. They reach up out of the water to snag my hair and pull me under. The river wants to swallow me.

I wake gasping for air.

My head is stuffed with fog as I wait, afraid to fall asleep again, until we leave my dangerous country.

CHAPTER 17

Dawn breaks as we climb on to the raft. Maria is still asleep. I hold my breath as we move out into the river. With each pull of the rope, I watch the Mexican shoreline approach. We travel straight across the river.

We are almost there.

Mexico!

We bump against the shore. I take Papa's hand and step into the mud that sucks at my feet. I expect the Mexican ground to feel firmer. It sucks at my foot like the soft ground around the burned-out village.

"There will be no more rivers on our journey," Papa says. He knows this makes us happy. I stay close to him and pray there will be no more coyotes with strong claw hands.

Now, we walk along a road away from the river. Before we have walked half the day, round a bend, a checkpoint catches us off guard. Papa turns, and we follow him off the side of the road.

My heart beats loudly in my ears when I hear the shouts for us to stop.

Uniformed men crash through the brush. They reach us and push us back towards the road with the butts of their rifles. Papa keeps himself between us and the Mexican soldiers.

Our Lady, protect us.

What will happen? I squeeze Papa's hand so that no one can take me from him.

The men herd us on to another path that takes us to a cinderblock building. We are marched inside. They open a cage and push Maria and me inside. A soldier hits Papa's hand and his fingers loosen their grip on my hand.

They close the iron door with a *clank* that makes me jump. Inside the cage other women, girls and babies sit on a cement bench or squat on the floor. We are closed in like animals.

I hold Maria tight. Papa and Manuel call to us from the other cage where they keep the men. At least I can hear them. They will hear me, too, if I call to them.

"Don't worry," a woman says, in words that say she is from the city. "We will not be here long. When the *federales* catch enough of us, they will give us a ride back to the border. Until then, we can rest our feet."

Back to the border?

The woman's chatter while she cleans the rim of the white latrine bowl distracts me. The foul smell in the cage makes me refuse the *tortilla* she offers.

More women and girls join us.

I look for the boy from the bus as the men and boys pass by on their way to the other cage. I would like to thank him for his help.

And then I think about people who are paid to wait. I pretend someone will give me *quetzal*s to sit here in this jail waiting for someone else to be sent back.

Women and girls continue to join us in groups of two or three. The two benches fill. The new ones sit on the floor. A woman stands right in front of me. She smells sour, and trembles.

I stand up. The woman next to me offers to let Maria sit on her lap. The trembling woman accepts the seat and I pretend I will be paid more to stand and wait than I will to sit. Maybe I could demand the money be paid in *pesos* instead of *quetzal*s.

Thud, thud, thud, thud. The guard bangs on the bars with a stick. Maria starts to cry and reaches for me. I hold her tight.

"Come on. *Vamos*," he calls to us, as he puts the key in the door. Those who had the good fortune of a seat, stand. The *federale* swings open the door of bars and points us towards the open door of the building.

Outside, another one points us towards the yawning back of a truck.

On the truck, Papa and Manuel squeeze by some of the women to join Maria and me. I breathe more easily when Papa puts his arm around my shoulder.

"We will not have to start all over again. Only from the border," he whispers.

I will be braver this time. The truck sways and sputters on the way back to the bridge. When it stops, we wait our turn to climb down. We all walk back together over the long bridge that crosses the river.

When we reach the end again, the woman from the cage says *"Buena suerte."* She waves as we part, *"Que te vaya bien."*

"K'awilawib," I tell her.

We know what awaits us at the river. We thank her for wishing us luck, and ask her to take care.

☼ ☼ ☼

We have no money to pay the coyotes to take us across again. Papa must try to find work that will earn him enough money.

In a secluded spot protected by brush, we wait while Papa searches. He comes back that evening to tell us about the owner of a house who takes in travellers. The owner will pay me to work at the house while Papa gathers firewood to sell.

We walk to a white house with many rooms. The woman of the house does not let us inside. She points to a spot under a tree at the back.

"Your sister and brother can wait for you there," she says. "Be sure they don't get in the way and keep you from your work."

Manuel and Maria sit where I can keep my eye on them as I wash sheets and clothes in large tubs nearby. I scrub until my hands feel soggy. I wring the cloth to make it lighter to hang up to dry. I work until my arms feel as weak as the worms that tunnel in the earth.

Each night, before he tells us a story, Papa counts the money. And each night I wake feeling the hand of the coyote on my arm. I am too tired to pull away. I am able to slow my heart only when I realise it is just a dream.

✿ ✿ ✿

After weeks, Papa tells us, "Tonight we go."

CHAPTER 18

The camp of the coyote stands in a new place further along the river. The people waiting have not yet trampled the grass.

While we wait, I stare at the water rushing past us. When Papa picks up Maria, I shake Manuel's back. We follow Papa to the raft. It is our turn. I chase the image of myself splashing into the water from my mind.

Our Mother, carry us safely across, I whisper into Maria's ear. I teach her to pray in the way Mama and Abuela taught me.

The tug on the rope from the Mexican side comes in firm strokes. The raft glides over the water almost as quickly as I hoped. This third crossing was like the Trinity; Father, Son and Holy Ghost all working together for a miracle.

Once again, I scramble off the boards and on to Mexican soil. I turn my back on this river, hoping never to see her again.

We move quickly over ground we have already

travelled. We travel so lightly because everything but the clothes we are wearing floated away down that river. And as Felipe said, the sooner we get away from the border, the better.

Papa slows his steps long before the road turns towards the checkpoint. People at the camp told him what to look for. They did not tell us, only Papa, in case we are stopped, so that Manuel and I cannot tell what we do not know.

But it is not long before Papa looks both ways, to be sure no one notices, and he signals us to move off the road just past a large rock. We circle around the rock and find a path that leads us past several fields, to another path.

We walk in the *bosque* on the other side of a sandy wash, where water flows during rain. The trees hide us. The green shelter reminds me of our highlands. I yearn to be there, even as our steps take us farther away from her. No. That is not right. The place I miss does not exist any more.

Each day, as we walk, we are closer to Mexico City. The sun shines less through the thick, dirty air. Fewer stars show themselves at night. Papa's pockets are empty. We have no money for buses and have to rely on the kindness of people for water. Twice Papa has helped someone in exchange for *tortillas*.

The sun is about to leave us on our third day

in Mexico. My feet ache. I hope we will soon find a place to stop for the night.

Beep! A truck sounding its horn makes me trip on my own feet. Manuel catches my arm and steadies me. The truck slows ahead of us and pulls over to the side of the road. The driver gets out and walks to the other side of the truck. He pushes his hips forward, as if he were urinating against the trunk of a tree.

"Stay here," Papa tells us. He walks towards the driver. The man stands up tall again and turns to wait for Papa to reach him. They talk briefly, then he follows Papa in our direction. The driver stops at the back of his dull, white truck and turns towards the door.

Papa walks towards us. He bends down to pick up Maria. "We will ride the rest of the way," he says, and we walk towards the dark opening at the back of the truck.

I am tired, but I would rather walk than climb into the back of that truck.

Nuestra Madre, keep us safe.

❁ ❁ ❁

We squeeze into a small space, wedged between the heavy wooden boxes and the truck's metal side. When the truck lurches forward, I push my palms against the side behind me, to brace myself.

We glide over roads that would take us days to cover on foot.

Our Lady, could Mama and Carlos be waiting for us in the city?

I can almost relax enough to fall asleep standing up. *In my dream, we ride in the belly of a beast. How will we get out? Will we be smothered?*

As I wake, the truck slows and makes a turn. Horns honk. The truck stops. My forehead hurts. Something thin and sharp pierces my skin. A scorpion?

I hear a door bang. There is a click like the pop of a match igniting, then a groan like a loud yawn. I know the back of the truck is open because the roof glows with light and there is shouting. I follow Manuel. We wiggle sideways towards the door. When I reach the opening, Manuel reaches out his hand to me. I feel Papa and Maria behind me. I know I should jump off the back of the truck, but I am startled by what I see. I pause, not understanding. The photographs Maestro showed us did not prepare me.

The truck is standing on top of a hill. Below us stands Mexico City. Even though the sun has just risen, cars and trucks clog her roads. People stream along with bicycles and carts. The movement flows through the canyons below us like paths of ants.

So many people!

Papa nudges me. I squat, then jump off the back of

the truck. Around us, engines hum like a giant swarm of wasps. Grit in the air swirls thick; I taste it on my tongue. The smell reminds me of the rain of poison on the grower's fields. The smell is so foul that my lungs do not want me to take a full breath. I wish I had my shawl to cover my nose.

Papa jumps to the pavement, then reaches up for Maria. He takes her from the edge of the truck and twirls her down to me. Behind Maria, other people emerge. The two men jump down and disappear down an alley. Two women head in the other direction. I did not realise that so many have been travelling with us.

"Get back in. We'll unload a few miles down the road," the driver says.

While I wait for Manuel to climb in, I feel my forehead. My fingers find a splinter. I pull out a sliver of wood. There is blood on the tip. I roll it between my fingers and drop it on the pavement, before I am lifted up into the back of the truck again.

✿ ✿ ✿

Papa and Manuel help to unload the truck, in payment for the ride. Maria and I wait huddled in the next doorway.

When they've finished, the driver waves goodbye, climbs back into his empty truck and drives away.

We stand on the pavement. People walk around us as if we were a boulder in the river. The safe place Maestro wrote down for Papa was in the backpack that floated down the river. Felipe said that parks are the safest places, so we find a green space – a park as big as our village. In the centre stands a huge white fountain spraying water. We sink to the ground, sprawling in the shade of a tree. Cars and trucks rush around the edge of the park. After a short rest, Papa stands up.

"I'll be back," he says. We watch him trudge across the park. He turns to wave. When the traffic slows down, he crosses and joins the river of people. The cars and trucks move again. Papa is gone.

We three sit and watch the parade of people and machines around us. I slip off my shoes and rub my feet. I put my shoes back on and lie back against the tree.

I am startled awake by Maria tugging me.

"Mano," she tells me.

I turn my head to look at Manuel. The grass bent and flat shows the spot where he was sitting.

"Mano," Maria says again, looking in the direction Papa went. I follow her gaze and see him.

"Manuel. Stop!" I shout at my brother's back.

He nears the edge of the park and turns to call back, "I'm hungry. I'll find some food for us."

I pick up Maria and run towards my brother.

I see him reach the edge of the park. I hear a blare of horns when he dashes into the street. He dodges back and forth as though he is playing football, dribbling the ball towards a goal defended by lots of other players. He reaches the other side of the street. I blow out air in relief. Monkey, I think to myself, grateful that he was not crushed.

I stand holding Maria's hand, hoping Manuel will not disappear before I can cross this street and follow. I see no end to the cars. Colours blur as they speed past.

"*K'awilawib*," a woman says. Am I dreaming? "Come," she says. Papa told us not to talk with anyone. I look at this woman's hand-woven *huipil* and skirt down to her ankles. She is one of us. Her voice echoes the highlands. She sounds like my mother. The woman's baby hides from view inside the shawl on her back.

"*Gracias*," I say. I pick up Maria and follow the woman into the street. We cross halfway and wait in the traffic. Cars pass so close that their wind touches me. My stomach turns. Maria hides her face in my neck. If I closed my eyes, would I feel less like a blade of grass in a field?

As soon as I close my eyes, I feel the woman's hand on my shoulder. I am grateful for her touch that steadies me while we wait.

Finally she says, "Now!"

We scurry across the street.

I can no longer see Manuel on the pavement. Too many people weave between where we stand and where he must have walked.

"This way," the woman says. She is not much taller than I. We are both shorter than many of the people on the pavement. But she seems to know exactly who Maria and I are looking for. She tracks him as though she senses him somehow.

"Did I hear you call him Manuel?" she asks, still looking ahead.

And when I tell her "yes," she calls ahead, "Manuel!"

He must have stopped, because in twenty steps we overtake him. He looks up into the eyes of this woman who speaks in our mother's voice and knows his name.

As if reading his mind, she smiles and says, "I am Juana."

"I am Manuel," he answers.

"Yes, I know," Juana teases. Manuel laughs. How long has it been since I heard him laughing?

"Are you by yourselves?" Juana asks us.

I shake my head. "Our papa is working," I say, and my empty stomach hopes this is true.

"No mama?" Juana says. She touches the hair

on Manuel's head and smiles.

"She left us," Manuel says. "She took my brother and left us behind."

Juana's smile fades.

"She had to," I say. Juana does not ask more.

"Let's go and find some dinner," she says. When I hesitate, she reassures me. "Down this street, an alley runs off to the right. There's a store that throws away fruit and vegetables that are still good to eat. I will show you where, and you can surprise your papa with a feast when he returns from work."

In my mind, I draw the details of the stores we pass, so that we can find our way back to the park on our own. But it is just as she says. We pull bruised fruit from a garbage pail instead of picking it from trees. "Let us see what we can find from a rich family down this next *calle*," Juana says. We follow her down the street, wondering what we might find. Ah, *tamales*, hard *tortillas*. When our stomachs tell us to stop, she takes us back to the park.

"See you tomorrow," she says, and walks off with her baby still sleeping on her back.

✿ ✿ ✿

We don't have to wait long before Manuel sees Papa and flies to meet him. I watch as they walk back to us,

Manuel's mouth is moving the whole time. Even while Papa is settling down with Maria and me, Manuel chirps like a bird. He tells Papa about Juana and the places we've been to.

"Look!" Manuel hands Papa a mango and pieces of *tamales* we've saved for him.

Papa smiles as he adds a *tortilla* to our second dinner.

✣ ✣ ✣

Each day my father goes out and asks for work. Sometimes he finds it, sometimes not. Manuel, Maria and I stay in the park, taking care not to attract attention. The fountain gives us water. The trees and bushes give us shelter to sleep under. Sometimes we find a newspaper. While Maria naps, Manuel and I work hard on our reading. Manuel likes the football stories, so first we read about the games and the players who win or lose.

When the haze clears, through one of the canyons of buildings I see the peaks of two mountains in the distance. If Mama and Carlos could choose, I think they would wait for us on one of those mountains. I wonder if they might be looking down towards this speck of green in the city now. I quiet myself, as Abuela taught me. I focus on my breath while

I look at the mountains. I do not feel Mama and Carlos there. If they had come this way, the mountains would have called to them, but I do not think they would have answered.

CHAPTER 19

Each day, when Juana approaches, Manuel spots her first and runs to meet her. She takes us for a walk and we go back to the park with food. Sometimes she tells us stories from her village. Even though our villages are both Mayan, not everything is done in the same way.

Today I tell her about our *fiesta* and how we made an offering for our most important prayers, how we burned Mama's thread and Carlos's medicine pouch. I explain how the prayers prayed at San Jose's feet were released by the flame. "They travel to God in the tendrils of smoke," Manuel adds.

"We do not do that. We only put candles at the feet of the saints and Our Lady in our church," Juana says. Then she smiles. "When I go back, I will tell my village about your tradition."

She goes on, "On All Souls' Day, we send prayers through the air, too. In our village, we fly big, colourful, round kites, tiny pieces of coloured crêpe paper glued together in the most beautiful designs. Oh, my husband works for months on his. He starts the kite in the middle and builds circle after circle, each bigger than the last. One of purple and yellow triangles, then a solid pink, followed by white and blue squares. Bigger and bigger it grows, with no circle the same design as another.

"Last year, his kite was taller than he was. And we write a prayer for those who have gone before us on a slip of paper. When the kite is in the sky, the message flies up the string and soars with the kite. My husband's kite soars so high that it looks like a speck in the sky."

I long to see bright kites against the force of a breeze. I want to feel the pull, the tug of the invisible. What message would I send Abuela on that string? My heart knows it is the words I have been praying for her each night.

Juana produces a comb. "Would you like me to untangle your hair?" I sit in front of her. The feel of the comb against my head, the gentle touch of someone pulling through to the ends of my hair, melts my worry.

I wish I had my backstrap, then I would weave the kite design Juana is telling us about. One row of purple and yellow triangles, then a row of pink, followed by white and blue squares. I would weave each row and give them back to her.

Manuel sits close, so that when Juana's hand reaches out, it will find him.

The chimes on the bell tower ring and Juana bids us goodbye. She has never stayed long enough for her baby to wake.

Each evening when Papa returns, he is surprised at what we have gleaned from *gente rica*, the rich people who throw away food. He has not yet met Juana, but his stomach and heart are grateful that we have.

That night, in the bushes where we sleep, I dream of circling kites with designs of grey and black and white. My kite tears and drops from the sky.

Juana appears. She dips a small brush into a jar of glue and wipes it on to a piece of green tissue paper. She hands the wet paper to me. I cover the hole.

✿ ✿ ✿

"Today is Saturday." Juana says. "When I leave, go to the far end of the park. You will be surprised at what you see!"

"What?" Manuel asks.

"I will give you a clue," Juana hints. "Today you will discover the sacred number of the Aztecs. Tomorrow you can tell me what that number is."

She hugs us goodbye and we turn in the direction she pointed out. Groups of other people walk the same way.

A man steps in front of us on the path. We have to stop abruptly to keep from ploughing into him.

"Be careful," he says in a familiar accent. "When you are with that woman in Guatemalan clothing, you attract the wrong attention. You'll get picked up and sent back. Danger lives here too." He turns and walks away.

Manuel and I look at each other.

We move again, following the crowd. I am lost in thoughts of my skirt that floated down that river. How I longed to wear it, to feel closer to Mama. But now, I feel grateful for the city clothes Tía gave us. We look more like Mexicans.

But what about Juana…?

✿ ✿ ✿

We find ourselves in another plaza. At the centre stands a tall pole.

"One hundred feet!" a man nearby tells his child. Towards the top, a crossbar extends out from the pole like a flat X. The end of each arm of the X connects to another piece of wood – forming a square around the X. The X in the square lies flat, like a table.

At each corner a rope dangles. One man sits on the pole above the X. Four other men sit, one at each corner. All five men wear bright white shirts, deep red trousers and hats tied under their chins. Each hat has a feather and colourful flowers and ribbons flowing from its top. The four hold on to the crossbar as the man on top slowly turns the X. I hope they're holding on tight!

The men slowly come down the ropes. The man still on top turns the X. The movement pushes the flyers out and away from the pole in a circle.

"One," people in the crowd call out, as the flyers complete their first circle.

"Two," they chant, as the men fly over us a second time.

The men flip upside down. I gasp, thinking they will fall, but they continue their flight as the ribbons attached to the top of their hats float out.

"Three," we count with the others. By the time we reach eight, my stomach is queasy.

Maria mimics the crowd, "Nine," she says in the pause before the crowd starts "ten". She says each number with great seriousness, as though her words are helping the men crawl down the ropes towards the earth. She speaks as though her words help them hold on even tighter.

"Eleven," the crowd says.

"Twelve." How many more turns, before the men's arms give out or they hit the ground with their heads?

"Twelve," Maria says. They are almost down.

"Thirteen." When they have turned around thirteen times, the ribbons brush the ground and the men flip back over and land on their feet, safely back on earth.

Just watching them has made me dizzy, and yet they can still walk a straight line.

"Thirteen. The sacred number," Manuel says. "We must tell Juana!"

Music starts to play, and I realise with the fading light that Papa is probably looking for us.

"Come on," I say to Manuel. Maria wants to walk on her own, now that we have separated from the crowd.

"What number will we tell Juana?" Manuel asks Maria.

"Terteen," Maria answers.

Mama and Carlos will be amazed at how much she has grown.

✧ ✧ ✧

When I spot Papa waiting at our meeting place, I can see worry on his face.

"Papa!" Manuel and Maria call out together. Papa's worried look disappears and he smiles when he sees us. He has good news. I can tell from the way he sits straighter and taller, as though he has dressed himself in hope. When we are together, he picks up Maria and twirls her.

"One," Maria cries out. Manuel and I laugh.

"Keep going, Papa," Manuel says. "Turn her twelve more times, like the flyers we saw!" I do not want Papa to keep turning her. I want to know his news.

"Eight. Nine," Manuel counts. "Ten. Eleven. Twelve. Thirteen!"

Papa and Maria plop down. Maria's head wobbles and she starts to cry.

I reach out for her. "Oh, Hummingbird, come and lie down and look at the leaves on the tree, until your head stops spinning!" I cradle her and wait for Papa to speak. I want to scream, "What? What is different? What have you discovered?"

"The man whose house I helped to paint this week came outside to talk to me today," Papa says. "This man knows the language of the highlands. He told me about a convent, a safe place for us to go. If there is room, we can stay for a while. But even better, they know people who might help us find out about Mama and Carlos."

"Oh, Papa," I say. "Could it be true?"

"We must take Juana with us," Manuel insists.

"If there is room, we will come back for her," Papa says as he picks up Maria.

"We need to tell her," Manuel says.

"You can tell her tomorrow," Papa says as he gets up. "Come."

I jump up. Manuel scans the park once before following.

We cross many, many streets. Mexico City must have been very hungry once, to have gobbled up all the flat land. We walk until dark descends. At last, we come to a quiet street.

We stop at a door where a dim light shines on the words *Casa del Peregrino*. Papa knocks. We wait in silence for someone to answer.

I count silently until I get to thirteen, my age, and the flyers.

Papa pulls on a rope attached to a bell. *Clank, clank*.

A moment or two passes. A small window in the door opens. I cannot see inside in the dark, but I imagine an eye staring at us.

The window closes. After a short delay, I hear a dull *clink* and *thud*. The big door creaks open just wide enough for us to go through, one at a time.

When we are all standing inside, the woman who has let us in says, "Welcome," in a voice that seems to be expecting us. The woman locks the door. She is a head taller than Papa. Short white hair surrounds her pale, wrinkled face. She wears plain, store-bought clothing and a leather strip holding a wooden cross lies flat against her chest. It is painted with bright colours.

"*Hermana*, Sister, I was told by Señor Lopez that you might have a room my family could use," Papa says. "We can work to pay you for your kindness."

"Yes, Yes. Señor Lopez called to say you might be coming. Only yesterday we had a family leave us. We have a small room for you," the nun says. "You are most welcome."

"Is it true that you might know what has become of my wife and oldest son?" Papa asks. He tells Hermana their names and when they left our village. He describes what they look like.

"I'm sorry, I don't know of either one of them myself. But we might be able to find out more."

Either of them? Thinking that they might not be together sends a shudder through me. I can't imagine either of them without the other. How could we have made it this far without Papa?

Manuel nudges Papa. Papa looks down at him with a question in his eyes. I wonder if Papa has the same worry I do. Manuel looks up at Papa. "Juana," he says quietly, to remind Papa of his promise.

"We are very grateful for your kindness," Papa says to Hermana. "And we do not want to seem ungrateful… but the children were befriended in the park by a woman who comes from the highlands of my country. Would there be room for her, and her baby too?"

Manuel watches Hermana's face. She looks down at Manuel and smiles.

"Yes, yes. Your friend and her baby can share a room with Señora Garcia and her children."

Manuel darts from Papa's side and hugs Hermana's waist.

She smiles. "It is not safe to be wandering about at night. You can invite your friend to be our guest tomorrow. Come, let's see what we can find for you to eat."

Hermana leads us through the patio garden. Manuel leans down to smell a plant.

"Ah, that mint has a cousin which lives on the mountains with you. It has tiny white flowers. Try a leaf and see." Hermana plucks the top off one of the plants and gives each of us a leaf. Maria chews it.

"Abuela," she says. I smile. It is Abuela who comes to my heart as strongly as the flavour colours my mouth.

We follow Hermana into a kitchen with a shiny floor. We eat beans and rice at a slick white table.

When we have finished, she shows us to a small room. She turns up a switch on the wall and the room fills with light. Maria stretches for the light and flips it off. We all laugh. None of us has turned one on before. Hermana turns it back on. When she has gone, we all take turns.

Even though we have sleeping mats up off the floor, we move the mats so that our feet point towards the door. Our shoes stay on our feet, as they have each night since we left Tío and Tía.

Papa tells us today's story. "And so the man came out of his great white house with a red tiled roof – a house as big as a king's. He called to me in the way of our mountains..." Papa tells this story so that he will remember it and retell it to Mama and Carlos when we are with them again.

I dream of Juana dressed, not in her colourful huipil and skirt, but all in white, wandering through the park, looking for us, calling out our names. Mama joins her. Together they walk down the fog-blanketed street, singing our names in a mournful way. They slow down and turn into a dark alley. I cannot see them any more.

I wake with tears on my cheek.

✿ ✿ ✿

"Be a help, Tomasa," Papa says after Mass. He leaves to thank the man in the big house. Then he goes to find work.

After breakfast, Hermana asks us to follow her down a long tiled hall and into a big bright room with other children whose shyness matches our own. Today we begin to learn the Mexican National Anthem. We mimic the words the other children are reciting:

Mexicans, when the war cry is heard,
Have sword and bridle ready.
Let the earth's foundations tremble
At the loud cannon's roar.

May the divine archangel crown your brow,
Oh fatherland, with olive branches of peace,
For your eternal destiny has been written
In heaven by the finger of God.
But should a foreign enemy
Dare profane your soil with his tread,
Know, beloved fatherland, that heaven
Gave you a soldier in each of your sons.

War, war without truce against who would
                                    attempt
To blemish the honour of the fatherland!

I do not understand every word, but some of the ones I do puzzle me. *War, war without truce.* I cannot believe that is what God had in mind for Mexico or for my country. I remember when my mountain was dressed only in peace. I hope that when Maria grows up, it will be peaceful once more.

Later I sit with a book in my hands. How long has it been since I drank in a book with colour photographs? This book is about Mexico City and I am struck by the pyramids they say lie on the outskirts. I would like to see the one etched with the image of a strange creature with the face of a *quetzal* and the body of a butterfly. I imagine weaving that design.

I think of walking from our house through the village to school, passing Doña Michaela boiling her thread yellow in a steaming pot on her *comal*. I imagine I can hear the music of Catarina's voice.

When our lesson ends, Maria stays with Señora Garcia and the young ones while everyone else leaves to do their chores. Hermana puts her arm on my shoulder as if she has read my sadness the way Papa reads clouds before a storm.

Being on guard on our journey and in the park has made me strong. But now that I am inside a walled compound, protected by a lock and key, I feel as though all that strength has broken off and shattered on to the hard tiles of the hallway where we walk.

Manuel and I follow Hermana to the kitchen. Another child brings lettuce that Manuel washes. Hermana gives me a sharp knife to cut up tomatoes.

As we work, she tells us a story.

"Many people from different cultures share this tale of an unfortunate girl," Hermana says. And she tells us about a girl whose mother died. "A neighbourly woman with two daughters befriended her and began to bring her little gifts while the girl's father was working his mine."

Hermana directs the other child to sit and listen with us.

"The father wanted his daughter to be cared for while he was away. He hoped that some day he would find a good woman who could guide his daughter as she grew. But when he met this woman, his heart told him that she was not the right one.

"Each time the father returned, his daughter told him how good this woman was to her. Finally, she thoroughly convinced her father. He buried all his misgivings and married the woman."

Hermana sets out a stack of plates.

"Now that the woman was married, she and her daughters treated the girl differently when her father was away. They were no longer kind.

"'It's not fair!' the sisters said, when they had to share the girl's bedroom.

"But because the daughter had persuaded her father to marry the woman, she did not talk badly about her new stepmother.

"When the father returned, he saw that his daughter was now sleeping in the kitchen by the stove. She reassured him. 'Father, I am happy to give my room to my stepsisters. And this spot is so warm.'"

Hermana's story is interrupted. "Food is ready. It's time to ring the bell!" Hermana says, giving the pot another big stir. "Manuel, will you ring the bell?"

"But what about the story?" Manuel asks. I want to know too.

"Tomorrow, *m'hijo*. Tomorrow," Hermana says and motions for him to ring the bell.

Clang, clang. As the echo fades, the children and Señora Garcia come through the door and find places at the table. Maria runs to me. We laugh and sit down. We bow our heads while Hermana offers a blessing.

After lunch, we wash dishes and clean tables while Maria naps on a mat by the door. When we've finished, Maria still hasn't woken up.

"We should go and look for Juana now," Manuel says.

"When Maria wakes, we will go," I tell him.

Manuel bumps a metal bowl on the counter. It clatters on to the floor. Maria wakes with a start.

I punch his arm as I go to soothe her. Manuel

and I, along with a groggy Maria, go off to search the park for Juana.

✿ ✿ ✿

It is a long walk. When we finally arrive, we can't find Juana and her baby. Manuel insists that we visit each of the alleys we have been to with her.

"Why isn't she here?" he says, for the tenth time.

"Maybe she is looking for us," I say.

"Yes," Manuel says. "She will look until she finds us."

"Do you think it might be easier for her to find us tomorrow if we stay in one place?" I say this as a question, even though I know the answer.

Manuel does not speak as we walk back to the convent. He kicks a bottle that flies into the street and shatters. Luckily, no one seems to notice.

"You little monkey! Papa wouldn't want us to draw attention to ourselves. Come along. We need to hurry if we want to get there before dark." I think of that man saying, "Danger lies here too…"

Maria does not mind being carried. Where is the pastry shop where we turn off? I don't remember walking so far. I don't recognise the buildings.

"We need to go back," I say. Manuel smiles.

"Oh, good!" Manuel says, thinking we are going back to the park.

"No Monkey, we've gone the wrong way." And so as we walk along the pavement, I pretend not to see Manuel wipe the tears from his cheeks. We walk in silence until we find the pastry shop.

With a sigh, we turn the right way this time.

☼ ☼ ☼

This morning, we learn more of the anthem:

> *War, war! The patriotic banners*
> *Saturate in waves of blood.*
> *War, war! On the mount, in the vale*
> *The terrifying cannon thunder*
> *And the echoes nobly resound*
> *To the cries of union! liberty!*

> *Fatherland, before your children become*
>   *unarmed*
> *Beneath the yoke their necks in sway,*
> *May your countryside be watered with blood,*
> *On blood their feet trample.*
> *And may your temples, palaces and towers*
> *Crumble in horrid crash,*
> *And their ruins exist saying:*
> *The fatherland was made of one thousand heroes*
>   *here.*

Waves of blood. Watered with blood. Blood their feet trample. I close my eyes. Hermana touches my shoulder.

"Time to get lunch ready," Hermana says.

While our shoes echo on the tiles, I ask her why we have to learn these blood words.

"If the authorities stop you on the next part of your journey, you might convince them you're Mexican if you can sing this anthem."

If they can save us going back over the river again, I will try to learn these words that remind me of things I would rather not remember.

"Can we have more of the story you began yesterday?" I ask, when we reach the kitchen.

"Ah, the story. Have you thought what might happen next?" Hermana says.

"The girl finds someone who will treat her better," Manuel says.

Hermana looks at me to see what I think. I shake my head, although I am hoping that the girl finds a way to stay with her father and yet be treated nicely.

"Well then, let's see if I can remember how the story goes," Hermana says with a smile, handing us vegetables to cut up. "Did I say the father was a miner? I am sorry; I've just remembered that he herded sheep. Yes, sheep. So when he came down from tending his sheep in the pasture far from home, he brought three sheep, one for each girl, his daughter and her two stepsisters.

"Now, his daughter treated her sheep so well that in time the sheep became fat and its coat grew thick with a fine wool.

"'It's not fair!' cried the stepsisters, when they saw how much more wool the girl sheared from her sheep than they had from their scrawny, dirty sheep.

"The girl had a generous heart and so she shared her wool with her stepsisters. But her stepsisters complained that she should give them even more.

"The girl told her stepsisters, 'I wanted to use the wool to make a vest for father.' She reminded the stepsisters how cold it would soon be up in the mountains.

"The sisters laughed at her. 'You can always make a vest for your father. We, on the other hand, must have the wool now for our mother's birthday tomorrow. We must trade it for the most beautiful trinket before the market trader sells it to someone else. Our mother has been so good to you. It's the least you could do for her.'

"And so, even though what the sisters said was not true, the girl gave them the rest of her wool. The stepmother was given the trinket, but she never thanked the girl, for she was never told of her kindness. The girl noticed that the stepsisters had also bought themselves each a bracelet with the money from the wool.

"The girl was distraught that her papa would be cold. She went outside and looked up into the sky and prayed to Our Lady."

Hermana takes off her storytelling voice. "But now, *niños*, we must stop. You will have to wait until tomorrow to hear if *Nuestra Madre* hears her prayers."

As Manuel rings the bell to summon the others to lunch, I wonder if *Nuestra Madre* will answer one of our prayers and lead us to Juana today.

✧ ✧ ✧

After lunch, when Maria wakes up, we walk the many streets to the park. We sit under the tree where Juana first found us. We wait for almost an hour. In my mind I draw pictures of the designs on Juana's skirt and *huipil*, as if my thoughts might attract the flowers and designs towards us. Maria gently pulls a small beetle from a blade of grass and watches it walk on her hand. Manuel looks east, north, west and south, in turn.

When I hear the bell-tower ring, I know we must return to the convent.

"I am sorry, Manuel," I say. "But we will come back tomorrow."

"Juana will worry," he says.

"Papa and Hermana will worry if we don't return now," I say. I pick up Maria.

"Come on, Manuel." I offer him my hand, but he gets up without my help.

☼ ☼ ☼

This morning we have less to learn. I am so glad we have finally come to the end:

> *Fatherland, oh fatherland, your sons vow*
> *To give their last breath on your altars,*
> *If the trumpet with its warlike sound*
> *Calls them to valiant battle.*
> *For you the olive garlands!*
> *For them a memory of glory!*
> *For you a laurel of victory!*
> *For them a tomb of honour!*

I think if we were returned to our home, even though we have been brave, there would be no tomb of honour for us.

As we prepare lunch, I hope that the story of the young girl who was mistreated by her new stepmother will keep Manuel from pushing us along in his rush to find Juana.

"Can we hear more of the story, Hermana?" I ask.

"Let's see. Where were we? Has the father given the girls the cows yet?" Hermana asks.

"Sheep!" Manuel corrects her.

"Oh yes. It was sheep, wasn't it!"

Manuel adds, "The girl was praying, because she'd given away all her wool and had nothing left to make a vest for her father."

"Oh, yes, yes, that's right." As Hermana gives us vegetables to cut, she begins. "So the girl went outside and looked out into the velvet sky. All the stars shone as she prayed. 'Our Lady, guide me so that I can care for my sheep so that it will produce enough wool for me to make a fine warm vest for my good father before the weather gets cold.' And as she prayed, Our Lady read her heart. *Nuestra Madre* plucked one of the brightest stars and placed it on the girl's forehead.

"When the girl had finished her prayer, she went indoors. When the stepsisters saw her, they cried, 'It's not fair! She is more beautiful than we are with that star on her forehead. Make her give it to us!'

"While the sisters held the girl, the stepmother tried to pull the star from the girl's head. But it was no use. When it was clear that the star could not be plucked from the girl, the stepmother demanded, 'How did you get that?'

"'I prayed,' the girl said. So the two stepsisters went outside to pray.

"'Give us a gift – or else!' they cried to the heavens. When they came inside, it was clear that they had been given a gift too. Not what they would have chosen, but appropriate, I think. Do you know what they were given?" Hermana asks us.

We both shake our head.

"Well, in the middle of her forehead, one sister had the horn of a cow." Manuel's eyebrows shoot up. I smile. "And the other stepsister had the ear of a donkey. As they tried to pull them off, the horn and the donkey's ear grew bigger and bigger. The girls had to hide them with their shawls.

"When the father returned home, a prince came to see him about buying some sheep from his fine herd. The kind prince saw the girl, who was now known as Gold Star. He fell in love and asked for her hand in marriage, and they lived happily ever after," said Hermana. "And guess what the stepsisters said?"

"It's not fair!" Manuel and I shout together, and we all laugh.

When we've finished cleaning up after lunch, Hermana signals that it is fine to go off on our search.

As we walk, I think back to my prayers.

No, I do not believe I have ever sounded as demanding as those stepsisters.

✧ ✧ ✧

We walk to the park in silence. Maria squirms to get down and walk on her own. I hold her hand. After a few minutes it is clear this will not work. "I am sorry, Maria. You can't keep up with Manuel," I say, as I pick her up again and try to catch up with Manuel. Maria cries.

"In the park you can walk, Hummingbird. Promise." I weave between people on the pavement. We reach the park and drink from the fountain before settling down in our usual spot, where Manuel's already scanning each direction.

"Do you remember the man who said Juana looked too much like a Guatemalan?" Manuel asks.

"Yes."

"Well maybe we should get her *ladino* clothes. Maybe Hermana has some that Juana could wear."

"I do not think the *federales* took her," I say.

"I did not say that," Manuel snaps.

"Maybe Juana's prayers were answered, and she found her family," I say.

"We are her family now," Manuel says.

"We are not," I tell him.

"I am her son."

"We have our own mother."

"She is Carlos' mother, not mine. And if she doesn't come back to us, Papa will marry Juana."

I will not answer such childish words. I will not think about Mama never coming back. What a monkey! If he keeps this up, he may end up with a tail, shrieking from the treetops for the rest of his life.

I snap my fingers at Maria, who is wandering around our spot, and she freezes. I clap, and we play again and again. She never tires of listening for the snap, and freezing. Her big brown eyes look into mine as she smiles after each statue pose. Manuel ignores us and watches for Juana.

The bells chime. "Time to go," I tell Manuel.

"I will stay here for the night," he says.

"If you do, Papa will be angry. Maybe we have not found her yet because we come too late in the day. We will ask Hermana if we can come back tomorrow in the morning instead of the afternoon."

"Promise?" Manuel says.

"Of course. Come on." I offer him my hand, and today he takes it. We reach the pavement and wait for the traffic to thin.

As we step off the kerb, I hear a cry swallowed up in the blast of a horn. Manuel and I turn to see Juana running towards us.

Manuel takes off like a bird flying to safety. He runs into her arms. When Maria and I reach them, she embraces all three of us tight.

And then, everything turns inside out. Juana is crying. Now we are the ones holding her, comforting her as she weeps.

"Thirteen," Manuel says.

"Terteen," Maria says, patting Juana's back.

Juana's shoulders slowly stop rocking, as if the flyers' number has calmed her down. She wipes away her tears. "No, *niños*," she says, shaking her head. "Four men twirled thirteen times each. That is the number that makes up the Aztec year."

It takes me a moment to think of four flyers spinning ten. That is forty. Three more spins of the four. Twelve. Twelve plus forty. "Fifty-two," I say.

Juana nods. "You are a smart one, Tomasa."

Manuel tells Juana where we have been. "You must come with us," Manuel says, "or I will stay here with you."

"No. You belong with your Papa," Juana says.

"I won't leave you," Manuel says. Does he think he is a boulder that will not be moved by a wall of water?

Juana says, "I will come and meet your Papa, but I have my own work to do."

As we walk, I am careful to show her the landmarks

so that she can find us again. Finally we stand in front of the convent. We ring the bell.

Hermana opens the door.

"Welcome. Welcome. You must be our elusive Juana!"

Manuel leaves us in the hallway and runs to bring Papa to meet Juana.

"No, thank you," Juana says to Hermana's invitation. "Once I have met their papa, I will leave."

"You are welcome to stay with us," Hermana says. She talks to Juana in a soft voice, as if she recognises something that I do not understand. "No one will interfere."

Interfere with what? I wonder.

I hear Manuel's footsteps in the hallway.

"Papa is on his way," he says, as he reaches for Juana's hand.

Juana kneels and looks Manuel eye-to-eye. "It is better for me to stay on my own," she says.

"No, please," Manuel says.

Papa appears. Manuel turns to him. "Make her stay."

Papa holds out his hand to help Juana up. "Thank you for helping my children. Is there anything I can do to repay you?"

Juana looks to her feet. "No. I am glad to be of help."

"Señora Garcia will be happy to share her room," Hermana says. "Or, if you would like to sleep under the stars, you can stay in our courtyard, or under the porch if it rains."

"Please, Juana," Manuel pleads.

"I will stay the night on your patio, Hermana," says Juana. "Thank you."

✿ ✿ ✿

The next morning when Manuel, Maria and I go on to the patio, Juana has vanished. Manuel races towards the kitchen.

"Juana's disappeared," Manuel cries out as he skids into Hermana.

"Is that so?" Hermana asks.

"Yes! She's gone," and now his voice quivers. I watch him struggle to hold back tears for Juana, tears he cannot spill for his own mother. "May I go to the park and look for her now?"

"What about your lessons? What about Mass? No, I think you will only have time to look for her… in the kitchen. And when you find her, bring her to the chapel."

Manuel smiles as he scoots around Hermana and through the kitchen door.

In the chapel, Juana stays at the back by the door

and does not take communion. Afterwards, as we leave for our studies, Juana prepares to leave. "I will return when I have finished my business," she promises.

"If you pass the house near the park…" Manuel starts to say.

"Ah, yes, your favourite spot. Let's hope they had *tamales* last night!" she answers, as she hugs Manuel.

Later, I tell Papa how Juana never lets her baby down from her back. "I offered to watch the baby while she worked in the convent garden, but she smiled and went off without answering."

"She is such a good mother," Manuel says.

Papa says nothing.

"Her baby never cries," I say, remembering each time we have been with Juana.

"That is because she is a good mother," Manuel repeats, without saying the words I hear, that our mother is not.

✿ ✿ ✿

Juana spends each night on the patio. She leaves in the late morning and does not return until after dark.

Now we have time in the afternoons to play with the other children. We teach them to play *electrizado* quietly. Instead of calling "*Alto*," I snap my fingers the way Papa did near the river. Since Maria's legs have grown stronger and surer, she wants to play more. The children listen for my snap. When they hear it, they freeze. The other children practise snapping so that they can make us freeze. Soon, Manuel snaps as loudly as I do. We have to watch Maria because her snap does not make a sound. We freeze when we see her fingers slip against each other.

Today, Juana returns early and walks through the patio while we play. She stops when we stop. Manuel smiles from ear to ear whenever she is near. He leaves the game and takes the page of the football newspaper Juana has brought him. They sit together and Manuel reads to her.

Tonight, in my dream, Hermana sits outside in the courtyard with Juana's baby cooing in her arms. Maria stands leaning over Hermana's back. Maria points up, enticing the baby to look where she points. "The hostia," Maria says, pointing to the full moon just rising over the patio wall. "The body of Christ."

✿ ✿ ✿

We have finished dinner. I am sweeping the patio, when someone tugs the street bell awake. The *clang* sometimes frightens me, even though I know it is often Juana returning at night. My worry that the authorities might find us here and send us back over the river never strays too far away. I move behind the arch and listen. It is not Juana.

"Welcome," Hermana says and hugs a white woman with glasses and long hair the chestnut colour of the bird who builds the teardrop nest. "You must tell me all the news over some tea."

Hermana helps the woman with a box. Just before they disappear into the kitchen, I peep out and see that the woman is wearing a stuffed backpack, green and red like the *quetzal*.

In a few minutes, Hermana calls, "Tomasa, I have someone I think you'd like to meet."

Hermana smiles when I peep into the doorway. "Tomasa. Come and meet Amelia. She has just arrived from *los Estados Unidos*." She takes my hand and brings me into the room.

"So good to meet you," Amelia says. The music in her light voice makes me believe she is glad to be with me. It makes me brave enough to look into her face. Her soft smile hides her teeth.

"I'm looking forward to meeting your papa and brother and sister as well," she says. "I have some news that I think they will want to hear. Would you find them?"

News? It can only be about Mama and Carlos. I hurry to bring Papa, Maria and Manuel from the garden.

"Hermana's friend from the north wants to talk to us," I tell them.

"Manuel," Papa calls. Manuel pulls a few more weeds, then he stands up and shuffles along behind us.

When we are all sitting down in the kitchen, Hermana introduces Amelia. "She works with people who help refugees find safety."

I wonder why people like Hermana choose to help. Could they be Our Lady's answer to my prayers?

"Do you know a woman called Martína who was travelling with a young man named Carlos?" Amelia asks.

I stare at the floor. My throat tightens.

Papa does not answer. His eyes fill with tears and he nods his head as if he is wrestling with himself.

"Your wife and son are safe."

"*Gracias*. Thank you for this news," Papa says.

My mother and Carlos have crossed to the north! They are safe in Phoenix, a city named after a bird that Amelia says rose out of its own ashes. Mama and Carlos are safe. And we may be leaving soon to join them. *Gracias, Our Lady.*

"They will be relieved to find that you are here and well. Word reached us about your village," Amelia says. I look down. "And your mother has been very worried."

I hope she does not say any more in front of Manuel.

✿ ✿ ✿

Amelia explains that she must write down things Papa tells her. She asks me to take Manuel and Maria to our room. Before we leave, I see Papa hand Hermana the threatening letters that he had sewn into his trousers. When we first arrived, Hermana had helped Papa glue down the wavy letters the river loosened from the paper.

We three fall asleep before Papa returns.

In my dream, Mama and Carlos open our door. They do not see us in the dark and call out our names. They close the door again. I try to scream out, "We are here," but they do not come back.

I wake up and turn on the light.

✿ ✿ ✿

This morning, after breakfast, Amelia says, "Would you mind helping me this morning instead of doing your lessons?"

Once we settle down at the kitchen table, she hands me a box. Inside are sticks of colour she shows me how to use. The colours sing brightly.

"Would you draw your village for me?"

Even though there is a blue and a green, a yellow and an orange, I pick up the black.

I draw my village as it looked before the trouble. I hand it to Amelia.

"Is this your field?" She asks. "What did you grow?"

When I answer, she asks me more questions about the church, the place where we washed clothes and our house.

"Could you show me how it looked when you left?" she asks.

I hesitate.

"It's OK to show me," Amelia reassures me, as she offers another piece of paper.

I pick up the black stick. I draw the helicopter and the dead people lying like bundles on the ground.

I put down the black stick and pick up the red. I show her the fire that ate our house. I draw red puddles around the bundles. I draw Abuela in the field and put down the stick.

Tears spill on to my paper. Amelia rocks me as I cry.

✿ ✿ ✿

We have not seen Juana in two days. As we finish

our evening meal, Manuel says that he wants to search for her in the morning.

"It wouldn't be a good idea," Hermana says.

I begin to worry that Manuel might take matters into his own hands and disappear again.

Papa comes back late from work.

I walk over to where Manuel sits at the edge of the patio. I touch his shoulder and he joins me. Maria has already rushed to Papa, who carries her back to our room for a story.

When we've settled in there and Papa is about to begin, the bell *clangs*. I hope it is Juana.

Manuel bolts. He returns triumphant.

"Juana is back!" he announces. "Can she come and listen to the story too?" Papa nods, and Manuel disappears again.

When he does not return, Papa sends me to find him. I am not surprised to see Juana sitting on the ground near the garden, rocking Manuel. I know he does not share our happiness about Mama and Carlos.

He stops crying when he sees me.

"Our mama and brother have been found," I tell Juana.

"Yes. I have heard this happy news," Juana says. "She is a lucky woman, for whom I have been praying every day." She smoothes Manuel's hair.

"I will miss you."

"I will stay with Juana when you leave," Manuel tells me, sitting up.

Juana looks into Manuel's face and shakes her head. "You will go," Juana says. "You four will travel together like the four flyers who soar through the air. It would be wrong without all of you."

"I don't care," Manuel says, sounding more and more like the city people.

"Your mother needs you, just as I need my children." Juana helps him dry his face.

Manuel sits up with a question in his face. The same question I want to ask. Before either of us can speak, Juana says, "Sons and daughters belong with their parents. You belong with your mother." She helps him up and leads us back to our family's room.

She stands in the open doorway while Papa tells the story of the tiny wasps that conquered the mighty jaguars. Juana has a faraway look on her face long before the story ends.

CHAPTER 21

In the night, I dream that Mama and Carlos fly on the phoenix which rises from our village's ashes. When I hear a scream, I worry the bird will drop them just as Vulture dropped inconsiderate Toad in Papa's story.

Am I dreaming? Someone brushes past me. In the darkness, I can see a small shadow slip through the door. Another scream pierces the air and sends goose bumps up and down my body.

Papa turns on the light, and we see that Manuel's mat is empty. Papa rushes out of the room. When the shriek comes again, I hear Hermana's footsteps hurrying down the hall. I pick up the sleeping Maria and follow.

In the light of a host moon, as in my dream, I see Manuel standing beside Juana, who is on her knees. Hermana holds her shoulders and rocks her back and forth, rubbing her hand across Juana's empty back.

When the rocking slows, Juana looks down at

the baby in her arms. She shrieks.

Every hair on my arms stands on end. I move closer, in the hope that I can see the face of her baby and be proved wrong.

Juana's cries wake Maria in my arms. She starts to whimper. Señora Garcia arrives and kneels on the other side of Juana. The three sway together. Hermana and Señora murmur to her. Hermana smoothes Juana's hair.

When my fears are confirmed, I look up to see that Manuel has also seen and is slowly backing away from Juana. Papa and Amelia stand close by.

Juana has no baby. Instead, she holds a cloth doll against her chest and wails, as if she has only just discovered that her baby is gone and all this time she has been carrying this imposter.

I follow Manuel back to our room. He huddles in the corner, pushing my hand away when I reach to comfort him. A few minutes later, the cries in the courtyard stop. Soon we hear a gentle knock at the door.

I open the door a crack and see it is Hermana. I let her in.

"Your Papa will be a few minutes more. Would you mind if I stay with you until he comes back?"

Manuel says nothing.

"We're happy to have you here," I say. Maria

loosens her fists on my shoulders.

Hermana uses her storytelling voice. "When I visited a clinic in your country, I saw a nut-coloured bird with a bright yellow tail who builds a nest like a tear-drop." When she says this, I see the nest whose image I have woven into a belt. "Do you know the bird, Manuel? The one that gurgles and makes squeaky *woik-woiks*?"

Manuel nods and makes a cooing noise.

Hermana smiles. "Yes, it coos, and sometimes it makes a gruff clucking, *kyuk kyuk*... So you know this bird. They live in small groups and sometimes they live in large flocks, as people sometimes live in villages or cities. No matter where they live, the birds all have orange-tipped bills, just as people all have hearts. If you came upon a pair of these birds, you might notice the female working hard to build a nest. Then you might notice a male swoop down and pull on that nest. He might use his beak to poke it.

"If you did not know these birds, you might think the male's behaviour was mean. He might appear malicious. But that's not true. He is testing the nest to be sure it is strong enough to hold the eggs that will soon be laid."

Hermana rubs Manuel's back up and down, as if her touch underlines what she is saying. "We cannot always know the reason for what we see. We cannot know the terror that Juana fled from. We cannot possibly understand the burden she carries. Yet you know her enough to know it would not have been easy for her to leave her children."

Maria has curled up on the bed. Her eyes flutter. Soon she will be asleep.

On the paper that Amelia gave us, I draw my mother and Abuela. Next to them, hanging from a branch, a bird hangs on to the side of a nest.

Hermana continues. "It is difficult to be a parent and have to do what the world might think is mean or wrong, and leave a child behind. But we know that sometimes parents must do what might hurt themselves, in order to protect their children – just as your mama and Juana had to do. Tonight, Juana let herself think for a moment of the happiness that will soon visit your mama, a happiness Juana can never know."

Manuel is quick to paint some hope into the picture. "Maybe her children will find her."

"No, Manuel," Hermana says in a voice whose sadness covers us.

"After Juana left her village, her children were killed," Hermana says. "In a few days, your mama will find out that you are safe and have been found. The decision she had to make to keep Carlos out of the army and to protect you from the threats of those letters will have been worth the great sadness she brought on herself."

Hermana's words find their way through the maze Manuel has built against Mama's love. His tears begin to clean the anger from his eyes.

✧ ✧ ✧

As Amelia prepares to leave, she speaks to me in Spanish and some English.

"You must practise as much as you can," she tells me, as she packs her things.

She folds the letters we wrote to Mama and Carlos. She puts them away with her notes from her talk with Papa and our drawings, in a plastic bag. She folds the bag over and over to make a rectangle as long as a piece of paper, but only a few fingers wide. "I will tell your story to others so they will want to help, too."

She pulls the hem of her blouse out of her skirt and puts the plastic pouch with our papers against her skin below her belly button, covering it with her underwear. She tucks her blouse back inside her waistband.

I follow her out of her room and on to the patio.

"I'll send word, or come myself when it is time for you to come north," Amelia promises, as she hugs each of us one more time.

"*Que te vaya bien*," I say before she slips out of the door. *May it go well for you.*

I pray Amelia's journey is more than good. I pray it will be safe and that our story is put into the hands and hearts of people who will help reunite us with Mama and Carlos. *May it go well for all of us.*

CHAPTER 22

I have marked the days since Amelia left. The days have turned into weeks. The weeks have turned into months. Today I turn the page over because there is no more room for another stroke on this side of the paper. How much longer?

Clang, clang. I run towards the door to find Hermana locking up. Juana has just come back. Her cheeks are much fuller since she became strong enough to visit the city again. She hands me a newspaper.

"Thank you," I say. I hug her, then go back to the patio and lay the paper out to practise my reading.

When the phone rings, I run to stand beside Hermana. She shakes her head, "No," when she hears that the voice is not Amelia's. I pray for the day that it will be a nod and that Amelia will be the one on the phone to tell us that it is our time to come.

✿ ✿ ✿

Christmas arrives. I am so happy with the fruit and clothes Hermana gives us. I give Juana a drawing of the kite her husband made back in their village, beginning with one row of purple and yellow triangles, then a solid pink, followed by white and blue squares, and then I make up my own designs – as many as I can think of to draw the kite she described in the park. She cries quietly when I give her the *dibujo*. She fingers the colours of the kite as though they could bring her husband and children closer.

In the morning, I see she has slept with the doll.

As the New Year approaches, I think of the fire we used to build in our village in the plaza in front of the church. I wonder what special offering I might choose to throw into the fire. But there is no fire here. I have nothing to burn, so I draw on the paper Amelia gave us. I draw the fire that would help us start the New Year afresh. I draw Abuela and Catarina next to me, our arms outstretched as if we have just released our sacrifices. I have begun to dream of Catarina and Hector alive in the mountains. I pray that they are really alive and together.

New Year, 1985: I pray it will be a better year for Guatemala and for my family.

✿ ✿ ✿

I hear the bell and assume Juana has returned with newspapers she rescued from the park.

Walking through the patio, I reach for a few mint leaves to taste the memory of Abuela. Our days have fallen into a pattern of school, work, games, stories and the ever-present yearning that I wear each day and that plays out each night in dreams. I add a stroke to my paper. In the kitchen, I touch the number on the calendar that hangs on the wall and wonder how many will pass until Amelia sends word. I look to the edge of the pattern of our life, wishing to weave each line well, to live each day so there will be no mistake that would cause us to stop, to have to tear out threads and begin a line over again.

Each day, I think of when our family will be sewn together again.

I read from a Spanish or English newspaper, whichever Juana can find. While they help me with my reading and writing, I also read the news to try to understand the things that have happened. Things far away like the *Kongan Hab* storm, the fighting that is destroying our country. *Kongan Hab* are Tzutujil words I learned at the camp by the border, strong words that mean a heavy downpour. The rain that whips the wind and sends balls of ice down to pound the corn in the field. A rain that floods the canyons and streams and carries away the unsuspecting. *Kongan Hab* –

the storm that continues to destroy our people.

So far, the other threads I have read are too tangled and short for me to see the larger design they make. My family will be forever tied to these other threads that I have yet to understand.

Each night, after Papa's story, I whisper to my sister, "Soon, Maria. We will be with Mama and Carlos again soon."

✿ ✿ ✿

This evening, in the middle of January, with the taste of mint still in my mouth, I reach for the newspapers and my heart sinks at a headline that holds a word I have come to savour. *El Santuario.*

Throughout history, Hermana says, people have respected the sanctuary of holy places. Down through time, brave people of faith like Amelia and her friends have helped others more vulnerable. But here on this page, it says that yesterday people have been arrested for helping Central Americans. I read through the story. Phoenix... Tucson... Underground railroad... Co-conspirators... Priests... Nuns... Ministers... Women and men who helped refugees...

The newspaper in my hands trembles. I remember the feel of the cut letters glued on to the paper. I hear the murmur of threats wrapped around a rock and thrown at the wall of our *ni'tzja*.

I finally take in a deep breath and seek out Hermana to show her what I have found.

When she finishes reading the story to Papa, Hermana says, "It's time to call Tucson."

I stand next to her as she dials a number that I read to her from a slip of paper.

"Is Amelia there?" Hermana asks into the phone. "Thank you."

She looks at Papa and then at me. She stands and talks as though she is certain the muddy water will settle and be clear again. She puts her free arm around my shoulder as we wait together.

"Yes, thank you. I understand you must be busy, but I would appreciate you taking a message for her."

Another pause.

"Yes, thank you. Would you tell her that we are getting her furniture ready for shipment because we cannot store it any longer."

What is she talking about? Furniture? What furniture?

"It's exactly as she ordered. We have a large lamp, two medium-sized and a small one. It's been inspected and it's all in good order."

In the silence that follows, I understand. Papa is the large lamp, Maria the small one. Manuel and I are the medium-sized.

"I'd appreciate it, and I'll look forward to hearing what address these should be shipped to… Thank you. Goodbye."

Hermana releases me, so she can look at both Papa's and my face. "I hope we will know something tomorrow. You must be ready to go."

Papa and I return to our room.

"Manuel, we must get ready to move."

Manuel is happy to hear that we're going. He wants to wipe out the bad feelings he allowed to grow between him and Mama. Even though Mama does not know about these bad feelings, I suspect that he is as anxious to leave as I am. He needs to let Mama know that he still loves her.

Amelia promised she would look into Juana's case as well. Will the arrests I read about in the newspaper keep Juana from following us? Will those events in the north keep us from what we hope for?

My dreams shout. Men in black uniform chase us. We run through crumpled newspapers. Jail doors slam shut and toilets smell of vomit.

✿✿✿

In the morning, before I settle in the classroom, Hermana sends for me.

"Quickly, find your papa."

I race outside and down the street in the direction I know Papa walks. He has worked at the same factory for the last two months. Then I see him in front of me, dressed in his blue jeans and plaid shirt, his hat perched on his head. I reach for his hand.

The strange man is as startled as I am. "Sorry," I say to the man who is not Papa. I run on, moving between people like a thread through the warp strings, until I reach the great doors of the factory. I am out of breath.

The man at the door will not let me in.

"I must find my papa," I tell the man. "It's an emergency."

"Can it wait until tonight?" the man half-asks, half-tells me.

"No. My…" I do not want to say anything that would bring bad things to our family. "Abuela is very sick." Then I tell the man Papa's name.

"Do you know him?" the man asks the next worker who arrives. The man shakes his head. I make sure that the man at the door sees me, so he keeps asking the arriving workers if they know my papa, until finally one of them nods.

"Tell him his mother is sick and his daughter waits for him here."

"*Gracias,*" I thank the man.

I wait and wait. What if the worker forgets

to tell my father? Three, four, six more workers go through the door.

Hurry, Papa. Hurry.

✿ ✿ ✿

Clang, clang, clang. Papa pulls on the string. Before the last echo fades, Hermana opens the door and spirits us inside.

She locks the door and turns to us. "Word from the North. Your wife and son have been moved. Amelia hopes she will know where they are by the time you get there."

If Amelia does not know where they are, how will Carlos and Mama know how to find us when we arrive? If Amelia does not know where they are, how does she know they are safe?

"I think it would be best if you left today," Hermana says.

But I thought Amelia was going to guide us on this part of the journey?

We follow Hermana into the kitchen where she makes my father repeat a name and a number over and over again until he knows it by heart. "Just in case," she says. She takes out a map and goes over the route with Papa and me. "When you get close to the next border, you will be with friends again," she promises tapping the map at a place called Agua Prieta. It looks like such a long way.

Hard as it will be to leave these people we have come to love, we quickly prepare to leave. We spill many tears when we say goodbye to Juana and Hermana.

"I will take good care of Juana," Hermana tells Manuel and me. "There will not be a river to cross this time," she promises, but we all know danger lies between us and Mama and Carlos that could swallow us up, just as the river tried to do so many months ago.

I hug Hermana goodbye one more time. "Safe journey!" she says. "Our door will always be open to you." I know she means this kindly but I will pray that does not happen.

"*K'awilawib*," Juana says, take care, in the words of our homeland.

CHAPTER 23

We make our way north on crowded buses and noisy trains. This journey is different from our first one. Maria is older and can walk more. But she is heavier, so when she has to be carried, I leave her with Papa.

When there is a warning of a checkpoint, we walk away from the main roads. More than one thousand miles pass under our feet, or outside the window of the bus or train where I am rocked until I am half asleep. So many miles to find the people who will help us on our journey. The burden of knowing we could be caught and sent back weighs me down. I hear the warnings of other travellers. I know that bandits prey and that *federales* are hunting for migrants like us.

Since I have learned Mexican Spanish more quickly than Papa, I am often the one who talks to the bus drivers, market traders and villagers. I fight to stay alert, wrapped in my fear and worry.

When we left Mexico City, the moon was shy,

but now she is fat and plump. The land has changed, too. It is dry and brown with less and less growing on it.

"Where did the green go?" Maria asks. I am amazed at how she has learned to string her words together in Spanish. We have talked little in our language since we were in Mexico. Better not to do so until we are safe.

When we are safe.

Will we be safe?

If we find Mama, how we will look to her? I am almost as tall as Papa. My new blouse is much tighter. Manuel has grown too. But it is Maria who has changed the most. Her cheeks have thinned and, standing next to me, her head reaches as high as my waist.

The farther we travel, the less we see water. Sometimes there is not enough to wash, sometimes not enough even to drink.

Some nights, we sleep on the bus. Outside small villages we sleep on the ground with our shoes on, facing north. When we lie down to sleep on the ground, away from the road, I focus on the stars.

Tonight, Papa tells a story of jaguars and butterflies. The sky is not hidden by a canopy of leaves as it is at home, nor do the stars hide behind the lights and haze of Mexico City. They glow here in the dark sky like a bright promise.

Sometimes, Papa tells a story from our journey.

"Tell me about when I saved Maria and lost my 'ito'," says Manuel.

Papa smiles as he begins. "That night, Maria was so sick, she shivered like leaves in the autumn breeze. Then she shook like an earthquake. Abuela's medicine wasn't working. Tomasa gave her water and still Maria burned as if a fire was lit in her belly…"

☼ ☼ ☼

When we hear from villagers that there are *federales* close by, we wait until night to travel. We hide from the flashlights that sometimes search the darkness.

In the bigger cities I feel less visible, but I know there are eyes watching. I pray we look Mexican enough with our store-bought clothes and the round haircuts Hermana has given Manuel and Papa.

Will Amelia find us? Will we find Mama and Carlos?

"Soon," I whisper to Maria each night, "Soon we will see Mama and Carlos."

"Will soon be tomorrow?" she asks.

"Probably not."

In my dreams, faces follow my every movement.

CHAPTER 24

We reach Agua Prieta. It is so near the border that Manuel could kick a football into the United States. We find the church, just as Hermana told us we would. An old, wrinkled woman answers the door to the rectory.

"Padre Jesus is not in. Why don't you wait in the church?" She tells us. So this is what we do. Maria and Manuel and I lie down on the floor while Papa sits cross-legged so that he can turn to watch the door or face the cross.

I wake to the sound of the door creaking open. Into the church walks a slight man with glasses and a moustache. He wears a striped *serape*, but it is the axe he carries that catches my attention. I reach out and pull Maria close.

I expect Papa to protect us, but he has fallen asleep.

I am about to scream, when the approaching man squats down next to Papa and gently shakes his shoulder. Papa jumps up and puts himself between the man and us.

The man rises to meet Papa's stare. "I am sorry I was not here when you arrived. One of the elders of our parish was out of wood, and it will be a cold night for her to be without it."

I sit up. Is this the priest?

He leans his axe against the wall and pulls off his *serape*. He is wearing a T-shirt and jeans.

"Padre Jesus," Papa shakes his hand.

This is the priest.

"*Mucho gusto*, my friends. Dinner will soon be ready," he says, settling down on the floor with us.

My eyes tell him more than I wish they would.

"Don't worry," he says. "Good people are coming for you. Until then, you are safe here."

Manuel and Maria wake and Padre Jesus welcomes them. Before long, Maria has climbed on to his lap. After we have eaten, we teach him a song from our village, and he teaches us one from his, from the mountains of northern Mexico.

He bids us good night and we settle down to sleep in our sanctuary.

"We will see Mama soon." I whisper my goodnight to Maria, even though I am not sure it is true. The earth outside would have been warmer than the cold of this brick floor. But sleeping outside so close to the border is too dangerous.

I fall in and out of dreams where shots ring out, black blood flows, a spray can paints words on walls and stained flowers run. I flee from the fire of our ni'tzja as the sun peeps in through the window and brings me back to the safety of this church.

CHAPTER 25

We have waited several days, when early this morning, Amelia finds us just as she said she would.

"Mama," Maria cries, running to Amelia.

"No sweet girl. I am not your mama, but she is waiting for you," Amelia says, as she holds Maria. "Are you ready to begin your journey again?" she asks. I smile so wide, I am sure my lips touch my ears.

Amelia has brought us clothes. Brown and green. We change. We are leaving our convent clothes behind. "We will find a good family to wear them," Padre says.

"I have a surprise for you!" Amelia says. From her pocket she takes two small dolls dressed in a *huipil* and skirt for Maria and for me; dolls so small, we can fit them in our new pockets.

Manuel's face lights up when he opens his hand to receive a small red racing car. She puts it on the floor, drags it backwards and lets it go. Its wheels spin as the car races forward. Manuel laughs with delight as he chases it across the floor of the church.

We eat the breakfast Padre Jesus brings.

As soon as our stomachs are full, we hug Padre goodbye and we set off again. Even though we are only a short distance from the border, we must find a safe place to cross. It took us three tries to cross into Mexico. How many tries will it take us to reach the United States? If we are caught and can convince them we are Mexican, we will not be sent back all the way to Guatemala. I will not think about that.

✧ ✧ ✧

Soon we have left the houses and roads behind and are walking in the desert Amelia calls the Sonoran. When Amelia or Papa take turns carrying Maria, I feel as light as a bird. Amelia gives us names for every plant and creature we point to. Of course, Manuel is most interested in the plants. The *saguaro* cacti stand tall, like green giants. Some hold their arms as if they were waving. The round pads of the prickly pear grow in every direction. In Mexico City we ate the *nopalitos*, the new growth of those cactus. *Ocotillo's* tall thorny cluster of sticks reach skyward.

Manuel plucks tiny waxy leaves from a greasewood bush. He crushes the leaves and sniffs it. "This makes a tea," he says.

Amelia smiles. "Yes, the Tohono O'odham people who live here use it that way."

When we stop, Manuel pushes his car along on the ground. He turns it over and spins the wheels.

After a rest Amelia asks, "Ready to go again? We need to watch our time so that we don't miss our ride on the other side."

Otro lado. How long we have waited for the Other Side.

In the distance I see movement. I freeze. My heart races as I watch the tree to see what is hiding beyond it. A brown form moves again.

Papa sees I have stopped. He stops too. When the form moves, I see it is a horse. I can see the leg of the rider. Not a conquistador like Papa's story, but the leg of a Mexican *federale*. I snap my fingers.

Manuel freezes mid-stride.

Maria puts her head into Amelia's shoulder and grips her shoulder tight.

Amelia stops and looks. She signals us to follow. We move as quietly as we can down a slope and crouch, making ourselves small under a tree whose branches touch the ground. We wait with the lizards and birds. We wait so long, we become stiff and my muscles feel like knots.

Now we hear the hooves of the horse.

He stops.

He heads in our direction. Silence. He comes closer. Surely he can hear my heart pounding, just as I hear the sound of the hooves of his horse on the rocks and earth.

When I see the leg of the horse move past us, I think about weaving. I draw designs in my mind to quiet my heart. I draw the curve of Abuela sitting in our *ni'tzja* breathing that deep, calming breath. I imagine Mama waiting with arms outstretched for me. Smiling. My heart slows. I pray that the horse and his rider will be blind to us.

Finally, the hooves move off. We cannot hear them any more. Amelia stretches her shoulders. When Manuel starts to whisper, she puts her finger to her lips. Finally she stands up.

"We must hurry now," Amelia whispers. "Your ride can only wait until sunset."

A wall of clouds approaches from the south. They grumble and flash.

"Usually there isn't much lightning during the winter storms," Amelia tells us as we continue on. "That one is more than thirty miles away."

We scramble along an animal path, over rocks and around small bushes. In this desert the night gets cold, but during the day it is hot. I should be sweating with the sun straight up in the sky, but the air is so dry that I do not. I am afraid that will change, if the storm keeps moving towards us.

Amelia gives us a few minutes to catch our breath. We start walking again.

When we hear a helicopter flying low, we take refuge under a thick mesquite tree. It is good to be dressed in green and brown. The helicopter vanishes quickly into the distance and we walk again.

The storm moves closer. Papa carries Maria, and I am right behind Amelia, when she stops short and motions for us to squat down.

We stay close to the ground. We can hear someone whistling. My heart races. The thunder rumbles louder. The clouds block out the sun and the wind whips through the short trees. Its cold smell reminds me of the greasewood that Manuel pressed to my nose earlier.

I hear a voice singing *De Colores*, a song I learned at the convent. Amelia recognises it. She smiles. "Ah, a friend!" she whispers to me. "But let me make sure. Stay here."

"A friend, she thinks," I whisper to Manuel, who turns to whisper to Papa.

A fat drop of cold rain hits my arm, then another. I want Amelia to return. A flash of light, followed by a crack of thunder makes me jump. I lean up against Papa. Maria's face tightens and I fear she might start to cry. Manuel moves to the other side of Papa.

Another flash and crack. Now, small balls of ice fall along with the splatter of rain. They hurt my head. I shiver, as my clothes become damp.

What if the person is not a friend?

What if Amelia does not return?

Before I can take on that worry with both arms, Amelia returns with a friend: a thin, tall man dressed like a cowboy with a brown beard and moustache. He carries a large backpack.

As soon as he reaches us, he throws a brown plastic blanket over us.

"*Mucho gusto!*" he says as he joins us under the brown tarpaulin. He says "with great pleasure" as though we have already been introduced.

Amelia checks her watch, and says, "John knew this storm was coming and thought we might need an extra pair of hands, if the washes run with water. It looks as though they might, if the rain goes on like this." I do not feel good about what she says, even though the tarpaulin John threw over us is keeping me from shivering.

"If we can't get across before the sun goes down, we'll need to spend the night far enough away from the crossing so that we don't attract attention to ourselves or the trail." He speaks in fast English.

Another night? Please, Our Lady, stop the rain.

John's eyes meet mine. He pauses, then continues

in Spanish. "I have been rude. I am sorry. Let's see,"
– he swivels in his crouching position towards my
brother and reaches out his hand – "you must be
Manuel the botanist."

When Manuel looks puzzled, John explains:
"Plant man," and shakes Manuel's hand.

Then he reaches out for the hand of the wide-eyed
Maria, "and this is your sister? *Hola*, Maria!"

Then he turns to me, "And Tomasa."

And then he turns to Papa. "And of course you
must be Carlos the father, because you look just
like Carlos your son, whom I have had the pleasure
of meeting."

Amelia interrupts, "John has spoken to your
mother and brother before we shared your story with
the Sanctuary group." I am grateful our story was
in the hands of these two people, who found it to be
strong, just as a male bird might find a nest sturdy
enough to trust with its eggs.

The rain increases. Its splattering pounds the
tarpaulin. I hope the rainmaker takes off his drenching
storm coat and puts on a softer, mistier rain instead.

"Let's hope for a short storm," Amelia says.

"I have a rope ready if we need it," John says.

Rope? My heart races. Amelia scolds John
with her eyes.

The rain slows down.

"I think we'll be just fine," she says, looking at her watch.

I pray she is right.

CHAPTER 26

When the rain stops, we fold the tarpaulin and strike out again. The land was so thirsty that after just an hour, only the low spots still look damp. As the sun moves lower in the sky, we reach the canyon Amelia talked about earlier. I understand why we might need a rope. Débris from an earlier storm hangs tangled in the bushes and lower branches of the trees lining the stream. But today my prayers are answered, and we are able to step on rocks to cross.

Amelia checks her watch again and although she doesn't say "Hurry," with her lips, her body shouts *Keep moving*. Her feet say *Quickly now* with each footfall. All the adults take turns carrying Maria. John even persuades Manuel to ride on his back for a while. The shadows lengthen and the sun begins to set, turning the remaining clouds into a *dibujo* so breathtaking that I pause. Amelia grabs my hand and keeps me moving.

As we walk, the sky slowly loses the purples and

electric orange it has painted. We reach a barbed-wire fence. I would rather climb this fence than cross any river.

"Wait here," John says, and he disappears.

Please let them be here. If they are not, we will have to hike away from the border and wait until someone else is available to meet us on another day.

Please.

John returns. "Now," he says. Amelia pulls the strands of barbed wire open for Manuel to climb through. She whispers to Maria, as I release her, "my friend is strong, sweet one. He will carry you now." Maria climbs through.

Amelia turns to me, "Good luck, *m'hija.* The next time I see you, you will be with your mother." She holds the wires open. "*Que te vaya bien.*"

When I reach the other side, she adds, "*K'awilawib.*"

I start to sob from deep down. I turn to face Amelia through the fence. "*Gracias,*" I mouth. I do not trust myself to say it out loud.

On the other side of the fence, a smiling man named Jim directs us to cross the dirt road. When Papa joins us, we walk with Jim through the desert to find Doña Bernie, who is watching out for *La Migra,* the Border Patrol. The arms of the shadowy *saguaros* wave us on. I will weave them some day.

Finally, we meet a white-haired woman.

"Coast is clear," Bernie says, as we approach. She holds a sketchpad in one hand, and with the other she opens the door of the blue station wagon. Papa, Manuel and Maria settle in the back. I sit between Bernie and Jim in the front seat. Jim shows us how to buckle ourselves in and gives us all a bottle of water and *burritos*, which, he says, Pat his 'real wife' made for us.

Bernie laughs. "You are blowing my cover," she says. As we ride along, Bernie shows me her drawings. Even in the soft light of the dashboard I can see how she loves the desert. I can hardly wait to have pencils and paper of my own again. Soon I will set up my loom and put the things I have seen into images, patterns and designs. But it is hard to think too much about the drawings because the closer we get to Carlos and Mama, the harder it is to wait. We have waited so long.

As the road curves, a car coming at us from the other direction blinks its lights off and on.

"Let's play a game now," Jim calls back to Manuel and Maria in Spanish. "I'm going to ask you to lie down now and Bernie will cover you with a blanket and a bag. If the car stops, you must stay still and quiet as mice. Can you do that?"

"Yes," Manuel says.

"Yes," Maria adds.

"Would you unbuckle and climb into the back too?" Jim asks me.

Amelia told us we might need to play this game. Maria thinks it really is a game. I take off my seatbelt and climb in the back.

Papa and I curl up like snails on the floor, head to head, Papa behind Bernie's seat, me behind Jim's. Maria and Manuel lie down flat on the seat.

In a flash, Bernie covers us with blankets and a cloth bag. She leans something straight on my legs. It must be her easel or paper or the canvas of the painting she stowed in the back.

Jim keeps driving but in a few minutes, just when I am beginning to sweat under the blankets, the car slows down. I hear Jim roll down his window.

"Hello, officer. How can I help you?"

"How's it going?" says a deep voice through the window. "Kind of late to be out here."

Bernie jumps in. "I was painting. We got a flat tyre. My husband isn't as quick at changing a tyre as he was at your age."

"Thank you very much," Jim says, as though Bernie is insulting him.

"Would you be interested in buying a painting?" Bernie says. "I'd be glad to show you the ones that are dry."

"No, no. Thank you, but no. Stay in the car, Miss."

"Are you sure? You don't have an anniversary or your wife's birthday coming up?"

"Thank you, sir." I hear two pats on the car, like the sound Maestro made on the truck door before he left the village. "Safe ride home, now," the voice says, retreating.

Soon we are on our way again.

"You did a fine job!" Bernie says as the car picks up speed. "Just another minute or two and I'll uncover you." The weight on my legs is lifted, the blanket removed. Soon Maria and I are staring at each other.

"Soon," I tell her. She smiles.

"Soon," she answers. "*Tonight* is soon."

I climb back into the front and buckle up. Bernie puts her arm around me and soon I am dreaming of Mama, of Carlos and Hector, of Catarina and Abuela, Hermana, and Amelia, all visiting together like old friends in our village.

✿ ✿ ✿

I wake when the car stops. I look around in the dark for Mama. She isn't here. No one is.

Bernie opens the car door and gets out.

"Where's my Mama?" I ask.

She stretches and bends back down, so that her face is close to mine. "Ah, sweetheart. We are in Tucson. You still have a few more hours' drive to go to reach your Mama. But this is as far as I travel tonight."

Jim opens his door. "I need to check in before we go further," he says.

A few more hours.

When Jim returns, Papa is awake. "I need to return this car," Jim says. "You'll wait in Bernie's house for a bit until Ricardo arrives with his car for you to continue up to Phoenix."

I carry Maria while Papa rouses Manuel. We leave Jim's car carrying only the tiny treasures Amelia gave us on the other side.

"It was a pleasure to meet you all," Jim says. Then he gets into the car and drives off. We walk along the street towards Bernie, waiting in her open doorway.

Inside, in a large room, a television is on. I've seen them for sale in newspapers and in store windows in Mexico City. Sometimes, in the villages and towns on our way north, a television would be blaring in a store where we stopped to buy food.

Bernie invites us to settle down on a long, thick, soft chair. One is big enough for three or four people to sit on.

Maria climbs on to my lap without taking her eyes

off the television. The people speak English so quickly that it is hard for me to catch the words.

We have all taken a turn in the bathroom and had a drink. Now we settle back down in to the long chair.

The phone rings. Bernie picks it up.

"Hello," she says. "Yes, yes. Nice of you to follow up."

After a short pause she says, "Yes, thank you for arranging for them. They are quite wonderful and arrived in one piece, but I don't think they're right for us. I'm giving them to Ricardo. I have room for them here in my living-room until he can pick them up. I know Amelia has plans of being there when the delivery is made."

Another silence.

"It was our pleasure." Bernie hangs up the phone and turns to us. "A friend of yours from Mexico City wanted to make sure you were OK." She looks at her watch and smiles. "And if it takes Ricardo much longer, Amelia will win the race to Phoenix!"

"Come on, Tomasa," Bernie says, "You and I are the only ones not hypnotised by the basketball game. Let's play a game of rummy."

Now it is my turn to smile. "Hermana taught me that game," I tell Bernie. I do not tell her that Hermana let her Good Luck Bear sit on my lap. I became very good at rummy with that bear as a companion.

I can say all the names of the cards in English.

I help Bernie make hot chocolate. We sit at the table by the window with our cups. Each time a car passes, I pray for it to slow down. We play hand after hand, until the basketball game on the television has ended and another talking show has begun. When the phone rings again, Bernie just says, "Great," and hangs up.

"Another hour, and you'll be on your way again,"

"Soon," Maria says as she comes to sit at the table with us, like my own Good Luck Bear. With her next to me, I win a lot of hands.

Three fours, a ten, jack, queen and king of hearts are in my hand when I see a car approach, slow down, then come into the driveway. I turn my cards over without saying "Rummy". Bernie peeps through the blinds. I join her.

An older man with glasses sits in the small white car looking at the house, not ten feet from the window.

"Your chauffeur!" Bernie says. Then, after a moment, she adds, "Why is he sitting there? What is he doing?"

Manuel and Papa join us. Bernie says, "Excuse me a minute." She leaves the room. The car starts to back out of the driveway. Through the window we see her wave at the car. The man parks, gets out and walks up the path. He waves at us and smiles as he walks past the window where we stand peeping. He disappears, then reappears inside.

"What were you doing out there?" Bernie says, handing him a cup of steaming hot coffee.

"The broom by your front door is upside down," Ricardo says.

"Whoops. Sorry. That wasn't the signal tonight!"

After our introductions, Ricardo sits down and in a few minutes he has finished his coffee.

"Ready?" he says getting up.

How could he possibly know how ready?

CHAPTER 27

Ricardo pushes a button in his car and music with English words plays. Soon we are singing about spiders, farmers and mulberry bushes as we wind through the side-streets. We come to a main road. The whine of the road puts Maria to sleep again. Manuel and Papa and I play a game with Ricardo. We try to guess the riddles he tells us in English – then he explains them in Spanish.

Soon we see more and more lights. "Halfway there," Ricardo says. "This is Casa Grande."

"Big house," I say.

"Right you are!" Ricardo answers.

Although I see a long string of stores, mostly there is just darkness. Ricardo asks Papa about our trip, and I doze as the two men talk.

I jump out of sleep when Ricardo says, "Almost there." No one has to shake me awake. I watch the houses we pass. And before I know it, the car slows down. I see people standing in the glow of a light on the edge of the *calle*. I recognize only one: Amelia. As the car stops, the doors are opened from the outside.

"Welcome!" I hear Amelia call.

Who are these people?

I sit tight. Papa jumps out of the car. He lets out a sound I have never heard before, as though he has swallowed his own heart. He hugs a thin woman. Before I can see her properly, I whisper, "Mama?"

The woman's head wobbles in tiny movements on Papa's shoulder, as though she is crying. She releases him and turns towards the car. In the dim light, for a split second, I am not sure this woman with wet cheeks is my mother. I see a young Abuela. But in the instant it takes lightning to flash, my doubt dissolves like *dulce* left out in the rain. Mama pulls me out of the car and holds me tight. She whispers, "Oh, Tomasa, how I've missed you."

Nothing in my life will ever feel as good as Mama's arms around me.

Manuel squeezes between Mama and me. Sobbing, he holds her as though she already knows about his anger. His fists grasp the fabric of the back of her blouse, as if he were to hold her hard enough, she would forgive him. But at this moment Mama knows only happiness.

All the sadness of Abuela and our village fall away

in the warmth of Mama's arms.

Amelia reaches for Manuel and me. She points towards a man in the shadow. He steps into the light and my heart skips. Carlos! My brother Carlos.

Manuel reaches him first.

"Manuelito!" Carlos cries. He pretends to strain and grunt as he tries to lift our youngest brother, who is now almost as tall as he is.

"Manuel," he says to Carlos, "I am Manuel now."

Carlos answers with a smile. He shakes Manuel's hand and then catches him in a hug before he lets him go, and turns to me for my hug. When Carlos releases me, I see Papa and Mama are holding each other again. Papa is holding Maria, who hides in Papa's neck. Mama's hand caresses Maria's head. Papa's tears run freely and he tries to coax Maria to look. Finally she lifts her face to the cooing.

"Mama?" Maria says. "You are my mama?"

"Yes," Mama says. "I am your mama, who has missed you very much."

The others who have been watching us, move towards the house. One of the women invites us inside. "Come."

Marimba music plays. So many people shake our hands and introduce themselves! I cannot remember all these new names, even though they all call us by ours.

"Tomasa, I have heard what a responsible sister you have been," one of them says. I have a hard time keeping my eyes off Mama and Carlos. I keep looking from one to the other.

"You're as dusty as the paths we walked," Amelia says.

A bath or food first? Thanks to the fruit and *burritos* in the picnic basket Ricardo stowed in the car for us, and the hot chocolate and cookies at Bernie's, the choice is easy.

The water is warm. I have never before slipped into water filled with bubbles. I close my eyes as Mama makes little circles on my head with her fingers. She shows me my face in a mirror and I laugh at my soapy white hat.

She tilts my head back, and with a cup, she scoops out water from the tub and rinses my hair. She twists it into a rope. I reach out and stretch my fingers to measure its thickness before she covers it with a yellow towel.

When I finally sit at the table in clean clothes, the black bean *tamales* taste alive in my mouth. My stomach feels full. I find myself falling asleep at the table.

People say their goodbyes. Soon only my family is left with Barbara, the woman who owns the house.

"Anything you need, don't hesitate to ask,"

she says, after she's showed us how to open the long chair that hides a bed for Mama and Papa to sleep on. Maria and I unroll our sleeping bags while Carlos and Manuel blow into the mat as though it were a balloon, like the ones we saw in the park in Mexico City.

When we are all settled down, we let Mama pick the first story from the choices Manuel gives her: When Tomasa ran away; Tío and Tía; Going to jail; Crossing the river; Juana; Hermana; Crossing the line. "You choose, Mama."

I settle next to Mama, Maria on my lap. Mama reaches for my hand. I touch her palm with my finger. A red scar runs from under her thumb to the bottom of her smallest finger. She caresses my hand. "We have many stories to share and many nights together to tell them," she says, looking towards Manuel on her other side. "We too crossed that river. I would like to hear that story first."

As Papa describes Manuel falling off the raft and Papa diving to untangle the rope, Mama shakes her head from side to side and squeezes my hand, as if that could keep us all on that raft until it brought us to safety.

"Oh, that was hard to listen to," Mama says. Maria climbs from my lap on to Mama's. Mama listens as Papa finishes the story with her eyes closed, her head down so that her nose is buried in Maria's hair.

When Papa is done, Mama looks up and says, "Tomorrow you may choose one of Carlos' and my stories. Maybe one that is less frightening."

I will wait until Mama decides to tell the story of her hand. I will not ask. Just as I know she will not ask us about Abuela until I am ready to tell her.

✿ ✿ ✿

In the middle of the night, I wake to the slam of a car door. What if *La Migra* is hunting for us?

I tiptoe to the window, where the cat sleeps in a basket. I peep through the slats and see a woman dressed in white opening the back door of her car. She reaches in and pulls out a sleeping child from the back seat. She closes the door with her hip and carries the child toward the house across the street, past a thick vine climbing up a pole. The door opens and a soft light from the room spills out on her. She turns around slowly. She is so gentle. I think she does not want to wake her child. She closes the door and the light outside the house goes black. I picture her putting her child gently down on a bed.

I reach for my shoes, put them on and return to my sleeping bag. With my feet pointing towards the door, I nestle closer to my sister. I smile at the sound of my mother breathing in the big bed beside me.

Tomorrow, I will practise my English. I will write a letter to Maestro to tell him that we made it, even though I am not sure where to send it. Tomorrow, with Abuela, Catarina, Hector, my village in my heart and my family beside me, I will start to build a new life.

As sleep comes, I dream I sit at my loom outside our ni'tzja. Back and forth I weave. My fingers, like spiders, spin white paper which typewriter-men fill out, the black of their letters shout Liberty on the wall.

As Mama's song floats by on the river, my fingertips release the green of thick jungle, the deep blue of mountain sky, and the red of puddles spreading under the bundles on the ground, reflecting firelight, the bright purple, yellow and orange from Juana's huipil. I weave all these colours into a kite for Abuela.

I sense her there even before she steps out from the shadows. I see she has fixed her tzut *on her head as though she is ready for market. She sprinkles water on the floor as she approaches. The drops fall like small rainbows. Abuela smiles and reaches for me.*

As I release her from my arms, I whisper, "Que te vaya bien."

"K'awilawib," she answers. She takes the kite string I offer her, smiles once more and soars skyward until she is a speck against the blue.

ABOUT THE STORY

In the early 1980s, several countries in Central America became very dangerous places. What had begun as a suppression of the struggle for land rights escalated over more than twenty years into unimaginable violence.

In Guatemala, the indigenous people were targeted along with the *ladinos* who helped them. The Guatemalan government admitted later that 440 villages were destroyed during their "slash and burn" campaign. Human rights groups report that 626 massacres took place. An estimated 150,000 people were killed and 50,000 more were "disappeared". To this day, the Forensic Anthropological Foundation of Guatemala continues to exhume mass graves, so the true number of casualties is still unknown.

Some say the human rights abuses by the Guatemalan army took place to protect multinational companies' business interests in the region. Others say that the war kept communists from gaining a stronghold in Central America – which

United States President Ronald Regan referred to as "America's backyard".

More than one million Guatemalans were forced to move within the country and 200,000 fled Guatemala during the armed conflict. Many of the refugees fled north through Mexico and ended up at the US border. They needed protection because they faced certain death in their country. But the United States turned away Central Americans because they didn't recognise that they were victims of persecution, which would have legally allowed them entry.

Human rights activists volunteered to find safe places where Central Americans could live while they filed the paperwork for the refugees to stay legally. Some churches opened their doors to give refugees sanctuary. These volunteers, along with religious leaders from different faiths, founded what came to be called the Sanctuary Movement.

Volunteers drove south to interview and accompany refugees into the United States, organising a modern-day underground railroad to keep them safe. They then walked them through the legal steps necessary to seek political asylum.

The heroes of the Sanctuary Movement were ordinary people who made decisions that changed their lives. They risked their own freedom to save people they had never met, people from cultures whose lives were different from their own. They changed US policy, and now people from Central America can qualify for asylum in the United States.

I work at the Center for Prevention and Resolution of Violence established by the Hopi Foundation. This Center grew out of the Sanctuary Movement. Some of the people we help came to the United States from Central America. Many now come from Africa and other parts of the world. Some were tortured and all have experienced a traumatic dislocation before their move to the United States. At the Center, we help these survivors as they rebuild their lives. We also work with their children in a project called *The Owl and Panther: Writing from the Darkness*.

In order to help these people, we need to know their stories. The legal case for permanent residence in the United States is built around the refugee's story. These stories also help them come to terms with their new situations, help them find their voices and eventually heal.

Tomasa in *Journey of Dreams* is like many indigenous people who consider their families before themselves. They accept their fates and work without complaining. They do whatever they have to do to survive.

The threads of Tomasa's story were spun with the voices of many Central American refugees who came to the United States during the Sanctuary days. I saw Tomasa in the faces of children bent over papers at Owl and Panther meetings, writing poems and drawing *dibujos*. I tasted Tomasa's experience in the food we shared. I smiled and cried with children like Tomasa, teased them, and was teased in return. I listened to refugee children telling tales of their journeys.

I wove these families' stories into *Journey of Dreams* along with images that rose from pages of books, flickered on screens, and travelled on the voices of refugees and Sanctuary volunteers. These images haunted my dreams.

Tomasa's tale represents the stories of many families who were split up and forced to travel separately. Juana's part in Tomasa's tale represents those families who were never reunited.

Refugees from all over the world still apply to enter the United States. Some have to wait as long as a decade to get permission to enter. Today the borderland is more dangerous than it was during the time of Tomasa's journey. Armed smugglers traffic in human beings as well as drugs.

Tomasa is alive for me, just like the many refugee children with whom I have worked and played. She and all children who have fled from violence hold a special place in my heart. They inspire me never to lose hope and to keep working for a better, safer world.

GLOSSARY

abuela *Spanish* – grandmother

adios *Spanish* – (literally 'to God'), goodbye

ajchaquib' *Quiché* – people who work the land

alto *Spanish* – stop

amenaza *Spanish* – threat, menace

azadón *Spanish*, **azarún** *Quiché* – hoe, tool for working the earth

ay *Spanish* – expression implying disgust or excitement

burrito *Spanish* – tortilla-wrapped meal of beans, meat or cheese

bosque *Spanish* – wooded area

buena suerte *Spanish* – good luck

calle *Spanish* – street

Casa del Peregrino *Spanish* – pilgrim's house

casita *Spanish*—small house

catechist *English* – lay person who plays a part in Catholic rituals

chayote *English* – edible gourd

chilecayote *English* – trailing plant with edible leaves, fruit and seeds

coco *Spanish* – coconut

comal *Spanish* – outdoor stove made of rocks and bricks with a metal cooking surface

compañeros *Spanish* – male friends

coyote *English and Spanish* – person who smuggles people; animal of the canine family

dibujo(s) *Spanish* – drawing(s)

Doña *Spanish* – respectful way of addressing a married or widowed woman

dulce *Spanish* – candy

dulce de coco *Spanish* – coconut candy

electrizado *Spanish* – game where players freeze when "alto" is called

es verdad *Spanish* – it's true

está bien *Spanish* – it's good, it's OK

Estados Unidos *Spanish* – United States

familia *Spanish* – family

Federales *Spanish* – Mexican federal authorities

fiesta *Spanish* – celebration

frontera *Spanish* – border

gente *Spanish* – people

gente rica *Spanish* – rich people

gracias *Spanish* – thank you

gracias, Nuestra Madre *Spanish* – thank you, Our Mother (referring to the Blessed Virgin Mary, mother of Jesus)

grizzle *English* – fuss, whimper or whine

g'oy *Quiché* – guerrilla

guerrilla *Spanish* – group of people in Guatemala fighting government forces

hermana *Spanish* – sister

hermano *Spanish* – brother

hij *Spanish* – son

hola *Spanish* – hello

hostia *Spanish* – round, flat, white Communion bread used in Roman Catholic Mass

huipil(es) *Spanish* – blouse(s)

indigenous *English* – native to a particular place

indio *Spanish* – (derogatory) indigenous people

k'awilawib *Quiché* – take care

kongan hab *Tzutujil* – heavy downpour

ladino/ladina *Spanish* – someone with European and Spanish blood

libertad *Spanish* – liberty, freedom

maestro *Spanish* – teacher

marimba *Spanish* – wooden xylophone-like percussion instrument

masa *Spanish* – cornmeal mixture used to make *tamales*

mesquite tree *English* – shrub-size (up to nine metres) tree with edible beans, found in the Sonoran Desert

mercado *Spanish* – market

mesa *Spanish* – land shape with a flat, table top

migra *Spanish* – Short for 'Immigration'; the Border Patrol in the United States

m'hija *Spanish* – my daughter

m'hijo *Spanish* – my son

milpa *Spanish* – cornfield

mismo *Spanish* – the same

model villages – concentration camps where indigenous people speaking different languages lived after being forced from their land

Montezuma *English* – bird which builds a tear-like nest

mucho gusto *Spanish* – with pleasure

niños *Spanish* – children

ni'tzja *Quiché* – home

nopalitos *Spanish* – vegetable dish made from the tender new growth of prickly pear cactus

Nuestra Madre *Spanish* – Our Mother, referring to the Virgin Mary, mother of Jesus

ocotillo *Spanish* – plant similar in appearance to an upside-down octopus. It has leaves only during the rainy season

otro lado *Spanish* – other side, especially of a boundary between countries

padre *Spanish* – father, title used for a priest

peso *Spanish* – unit of money

(la) próxima vez *Spanish* – next time

que'cj a'k *Quiché* – rooster

que te vaya bien *Spanish* – may it go well for you

quetzal *Spanish* – Guatemalan bird; unit of money

saguaro *English* – cactus that can grow as tall as 14 metres

Santuario *Spanish* – sanctuary, sacred place in a church; movement to help people fleeing persecution

señor *Spanish* – Mr

señora *Spanish* – Mrs

señorita *Spanish* – Miss

serape *Spanish* – woollen shawl

sobrina *Spanish* – niece

Sonoran Desert *English* – 120,000-square-mile arid region stretching between south-western Arizona and south eastern California in the US and Baja California and western Sonora in Mexico.

tamales *Spanish* – corn mash cooked in a wrapper of leaves

tayuyo *Spanish* – masa and black bean tamales

tío, tía *Spanish* – uncle, aunt

Tohono O'odham – indigenous people of the Sonoran desert. Their name means "desert people"

tortilla *Spanish* – flat bread cooked on a *comal*, eaten alone or wrapped around a filling to make a *burrito*

tzut *Quiché* – traditional Mayan headdress from the Quiché region of Guatemala

vamos *Spanish* – let's go

vaya con Dios *Spanish* – (said when parting) go with God

verdad *Spanish* – truth

wash *English* – dry, sandy, low-lying area which runs with water during the rainy season

**MAP SHOWING
TOMASA'S JOURNEY**